THE ANIMAL LIGHTHOUSE

ANTHONY BURT

ILLUSTRATED BY CIARA FLOOD

GUPPY BOOKS

To my mum, Sheila.
Who lives, forever, beside her lighthouse.
A.B.

For Kay, whose support, kindness
and empathy has made all the difference.
C.F.

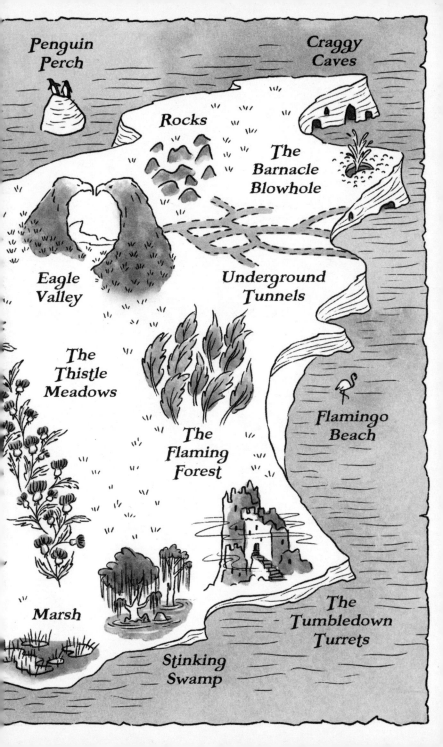

Yo-ho-ho, come float with me, across the sea,
In a barrel full of rum,
To a secret island, and a special lighthouse,
Where animals live wild and free . . .

CHAPTER ONE

It was a dark night on the island.

Moonlight rippled over the black sea, from the horizon down to Seal Cove below. Jim sat with his legs dangling over the cliff edge, a cool breeze flicking up the hairs on his shins. He listened to the growls and *aarf-aarf-aarfs* of chubby seals jostling for beach space, smiling at the thought of them bouncing off each other's bellies.

Grass ruffled behind him.

Turning, Jim watched old Oskar waddle up to the cliff edge and lower himself down beside him. The orangutan pushed his little round glasses up his button nose. He and Jim looked out across the dark sea, moonlight shimmering like a white carpet on the waves.

Oskar rummaged in a pouch on his tool belt and

3

pulled
out a banana.
Peeling it, he
broke a piece off
and handed it to Jim.

Jim curled one arm over his
head and rammed the banana chunk in his mouth.
Mushing it up, he stuck his tongue out at the orangutan.

Oskar snorted, slapped his knee and did the same.
Gooey, yellow banana dribbled off the end of his long,
grey tongue and down his chin.

They laughed, slurping up the pulp, as lighthouse
beams above them glided over the bay and out to sea,
lighting up Black Eel Rock. One, *swoosh*. Two, *swoosh*.
Three, *swoosh*, three and a half, *swoosh*.

The last beam was always a dimmer yellow, as if it
were an echo of the three before it. But it still lit up the

water, the light tumbling silently across the waves.

'What are you thinking about, Jim?' Oskar stroked his chin with long, hairy fingers. The old orangutan's furry head glowed with a moonlit, orange-white halo.

'I was thinking how we're sitting here looking out, but no one out *there* can see in.'

'You should be used to that by now.' Oskar finished munching the rest of his banana. 'I have explained how the last beam works.'

'I know. And I get it. But it still feels strange. How the lighthouse can *do* that.'

Oskar gently thumped him on the arm, and Jim sighed.

'All right, I was *also* thinking about how I got to the island. Will you tell me the story again?'

'It is getting late. Almost time for bed.' The orangutan shuffled around. 'And, besides, that story will still be the same tomorrow.'

'And you'll *still* leave bits out . . .'

Oskar closed his beady eyes behind his glasses. 'I have told you many times: we are your family. All of us, here, on this island. And . . . all of us,' the orangutan curled his arm around Jim's neck, flipping him backwards into an upside-down headlock, 'want you back inside the lighthouse!' Oskar picked Jim up by the breeches as if he was a feather floating in the wind and placed him down on the grass. 'Come on, it is your bedtime. And almost mine too.'

Groaning, Jim followed the orangutan back across the field to the lighthouse.

Oskar stopped by the lighthouse's huge black metal door, then glanced out to sea. Plucking a pocket watch out of his tool belt, he squinted at it. 'Trent is late.'

'He *is* old.'

6

The ladder creaked as it slid down on its Oskar-built metal rails. Wincing, Jim lifted his foot up to—

'Perhaps you could try and be a bit LOUDER!' A *tut* echoed through the darkness.

'Oh, sorry Rafi, I was trying to be—'

'The LOUDEST BOY in the world?' Rafi's high-pitched voice rang around the room. Then came the rustling, thumping sound of the raccoon plumping up his pillows. Smiling to himself in the darkness, Jim began to climb the ladder.

'You'd better not have eaten any of my cabbage this time!'

Jim rolled his eyes. 'Rafi, I *never* eat your rotten cabbage. It's the bugs from the basement, you know this.'

Rafi huffed, mumbling something about sharing rooms with a smelly boy. 'It's past your bedtime – *go to sleep!*'

'That's what I'm trying to do.'

'Well do it QUIETLY please!' The raccoon sighed and his voice softened. 'Sleep well.'

'You too.' Jim scrambled up, into the glow of his cosy hidden room, pulled up the ladder and bolted the floor hatch shut.

Yawning, he went over to his porthole-sized window and looked out, once more, at the dark sea. The lighthouse beams soared through the air, lighting up the bay. And, as the cool, salty breeze drifted in his room, he jumped into bed and fell straight to sleep.

At the same time, Oskar sat in his room, gently swinging back and forth in his creaky old rocking chair. The room smelt of grease and oil and – with his tiny, round glasses perched at the end of his button nose – the orangutan squinted, concentrating as he twisted a screw into the wooden handle of a long Charleville musket.

Oskar flipped the rifle over, remembering the day it had washed up after a shipwreck. That had been *long* before Jim was born. He closed his eyes and pictured the storm the night that ship went down. It had been one of the worst nights the island had ever seen. There had been nothing any of the animals could do.

He paused, hearing the memory of those huge waves crashing against the cliffs.

No one should have survived that shipwreck. Yet someone had.

He glanced at the young man's portrait on the wall, the one Elsa had trunk-painted so long ago now.

Stretching to put the rifle down, the screwdriver fell onto the desk and rolled noisily across the wood. It ripped the corner of a parchment poking out beneath a pile of books. Oskar caught the screwdriver and slid the old paper out.

Pushing his glasses up his nose, he held the paper near the flickering candle, reading the first few faded, grey words:

To Whomsoever,

It is my ardent hope that you have found my boy alive and well . . .

His heart beat faster. This note had come with Jim, washed up in a barnacle-coated barrel on Flamingo Beach. Twelve years ago. Oskar grunted. He crumpled up the parchment, shoving it back under the books, not wanting to read the rest.

Pulling himself out of the chair, he clambered up into the carved tree-trunk nook fixed to the wall near the ceiling. Then Oskar, too, sank into a deep sleep.

CHAPTER TWO

Pink-red sunbeams lit up one side of Jim's freckled face as he sat up in bed. He yawned, stretched and tumbled into the tattered breeches he wore every day, glancing out of his porthole window at the orchard Rafi looked after. It was full of apple, pear, peach, mango and banana trees, glowing from the sun's dazzling orange aura. The shadows of the trees stretched far into the distance, dwarfed only by the tall cone-shaped shadow of the lighthouse.

Scattered across Jim's room were old glass bottles, fishing nets, pieces of rope, rusted curved swords, water-bloated books and a pile of gold coins he'd collected from the sea. Some were from shipwrecks; others had floated here from far beyond. The island seemed to have a way of bringing things to its shores.

Springing to the bathroom, he brushed his teeth with a little bamboo stick with seaweed strands dangling from one end, humming as he stared into his room at the huge whale tooth hanging over his bed. Next to it were pinned scribbled sketches of inventions he and Oskar planned to build.

Splashing his face with water, the floorboards creaked under his feet. He hoped Rafi was up and out gardening, so he didn't have another reason to whine about the noise. At least Rafi didn't have to listen to Elsa's thundering footsteps above *him* every night—

Clink-clink-clink!

Clink-clink-clink . . . clinkety-clink!

Jim peered over the toilet rim. The noise seemed to be coming from inside . . .

Cupping his hands around his mouth, he yelled into the toilet bowl, 'Hell-*LO . . . LO . . . o . . . lo . . . oh . . . o . . . o . . . o?'*

Nothing.

The hairs on the back of his neck rose.

SCHNIP-SCHNIP.

A huge red crab jumped out of the toilet darkness and snatched hold of his hair with its claw.

'Ow, *ow, OWWW!*' Jim stumbled backwards, smacking into his sink, then, tugging the claw off his hair, he flung the crab on his bed.

'Cornelius, why can't you use the door like everyone else?'

'If you hadn't noticed, Jim, dear boy, *your* door is in the ceiling of that blasted raccoon's smelly lair!'

Jim huffed, watching the crab's eye-stalks wiggle left and right. 'But . . . leaping out of people's toilets . . . it's just not *right*.'

The crab's eye-stalks blinked three times. 'Yes,

I admit there is a *soupçon* of invasiveness about it. Anyway, Jim, my boy, my wife and thirty-eight children are waiting, so I shall make this quick.' Cornelius snuggled into Jim's pillow. He flicked out one of his mouth carapaces to clean his eye-stalks and idly scratched his shell with a side-leg.

Jim raised an eyebrow, tapping one foot on the floor. 'Um . . . you were going to make this quick?'

'I am. Goodness me! Children, you always want things now, now, now.'

A sour, fishy smell wafted through the window and up Jim's nose. 'Phwoar, those seals stink this morning.'

Cornelius raised a claw. 'Ah, yes, terribly sorry. That would be . . . well . . . *me*.' A gentle *parp* rippled across the bed sheets. 'Oops, there I go again. Just glad we know one another so well!'

'Shall we just pretend it was the seals?'

Cornelius's eye-stalks lit up. 'Oh yes, jolly good idea, my boy! And if Elsa could stop making her Brussel sprout stew, that would help, eh? Ha! Anyway, onwards. Where was I?'

'Making this *quick*?' Jim said.

'Ah, yes I had a message to deliver. Ha! That's the

trouble with having thirty-eight children and a wife
. . . you never get a chance to finish the thing you were
going to . . . anyway. The message is: *all the animals
are waiting for you up in the Lantern Room*. You'd better
hurry!'

Jim stared at Cornelius. 'Why, did something
happen?'

'Don't ask me, Jim, my boy! But what are you
hanging around here for? Hurry!'

Jim yanked open the floor hatch, clambered down
the ladder and disappeared.

Cornelius huddled down into Jim's bed sheets. 'In
the meantime, whilst you do that, I'll stay here. It was
an *ever so* tiring, and quite *disgusting*, journey up that
toilet chute, you know. And, to be frank, any chance
I get to have a break from the children is quite . . .'
The crab yawned. 'So, anyway . . . here I am talking
to myself, just like at home. And, I'm sure, no one will
mind if I . . . take a short crab nap and . . . fall . . .'

Parp.

CHAPTER THREE

Leaping up into the lighthouse's Lantern Room, Jim skidded to a stop on the stone floor, glancing at the wood-metal lantern frame towering above him, with each of the three bulbs inside its own metal cage. A sharp, orange glint of morning sunshine stabbed at his eyes, reflected off the huge Espejo lens.

Jim guessed the lens was maybe four times taller than him. Built from gold slats of mirror and glass, it spread across the Lantern Room's back curved wall, opposite the lighthouse windows. Jim loved its strange and beautiful distortion of things. The prism-slats folded into one another and, when he looked inside, his face, the walls, windows, even Claudette's cat-shadow when she climbed around the frame, bent and blurred and changed into rainbow-coloured squiggly shapes.

It made everything seem unreal.

And that was the special thing about the lens.

Its job, Jim knew, was to focus and magnify the bulbs' light into beams that soared out over the ocean, as Oskar had patiently, *scientifically*, explained to him many times. But its *other* role was to shroud the island from onlookers.

The lens' beams shone a fake, shimmering picture – for miles out to sea – of the island, moving its location around. And because beam three-and-a-half did something else even *more* special, to passing ships the island looked farther away the closer they got and then vanished, like a mirage.

Oskar had designed it like this for a reason.

Jim glanced at the canvas that hung to the right of the lens – one of Elsa's trunk-painted masterpieces. It was a painting of a young man looking out to sea, a makeshift raft lying on the beach beside him. Tallulah sat on his shoulder, her beak nibbling at his wavy hair, and the curl of a smile was just visible on the young man's face. Edward. Jim often thought about him. All he knew was that Edward had been a sailor stranded on the island for a while, long before Jim had arrived.

And, after he sailed back to the world beyond, Oskar had decided to re-engineer the lighthouse beams. The orangutan told Jim that, even though Edward had been a kind soul, and had helped the animals with their crops, they didn't want humans finding their island again.

Except, even mirror-lens mirages didn't stop babies floating here . . .

Jim spied Claudette by the door leading to the Lantern Room's outside circular balcony. She was rubbing her black, furry chin on the lantern frame's on/off lever, staring at Jim with her green eyes. The lever was in its 'off' position because it was maintenance day – a weekly event, every Thursday morning, when the lens needed dusting. And when, for the time it took the animals to clean it, the island's mirror-light disguise was gone.

The island was at this moment – Jim drew in a breath – solid and visible to the world.

Above Claudette, on the balcony walkway outside the lighthouse windows, stood the animals who lived and worked in the lighthouse.

He ran up the balcony steps and outside to join

them all. 'What's going on?'

Looking out across Seal Cove and Lighthouse Island's farmed, rich orchards, Jim saw deep swamps and forests stretching out below. Beyond those were its majestic cliff edges, and the choppy, ashen sea. A gust of wind punched him backwards, his clothes flapping around him.

Oskar's hair swished about like orange grass, curling around Elsa's trunk as her huge, grey ears threatened to smack Tallulah off her perch on the balcony railings. At Jim's feet, the three Rigging Rats, Rum, Flum and Sum, were huddled together. Maximus the millipede crawled across the window towards him, and Rafi looked at the others, puzzled, as his thick, white-grey-black raccoon fur – proudly unwashed for seven years – was stiff and unmoving in the wind.

'Look . . . on the horizon!' Elsa yelled over the howling squall, pointing her trunk.

Jim stared out but couldn't see anything. Oskar flicked open the spyglass and handed it over. Holding it to his eye, Jim saw a speck. It was far away, but it was clearly a ship.

He turned to Oskar. 'It's sailing towards Black Eel Rock!'

'We must log in the book what kind of ship it is.' Oskar pushed the spyglass in Jim's hands back up to his face. 'You have younger eyes than me, tell me what you see.'

Jim huffed; Oskar made them log *everything* in the Lighthouse Book. Jim never understood why – no one else ever read it. He looked through the spyglass again.

The ship's dirty-white sails were flapping. With grey-black storm clouds behind them, he could see there was something different about this ship. It wasn't like the supply ships, hospital ships and Spanish Armada galleons that he and the lighthouse animals regularly steered away from meeting their doom on Black Eel Rock. *Something* about this ship . . .

A shiver went down the back of his neck.

A tiny black speck at the top of the crow's nest looked like a flag. A black flag with a white shape scrawled across it. He couldn't quite make out the shape – but he didn't need to.

The spyglass shook in Jim's hands and he slammed it shut. 'We have to switch the beams on now, to hide us! It's a pirate ship, and it's coming our way.'

CHAPTER FOUR

Oskar stared down the spyglass's barrel, and a shadow slid across his face. 'We *must* stop that ship reaching our island.'

'*And* stop it being smashed to pieces on Black Eel Rock,' Jim replied, crouching to give Rum, Flum and Sum a hug – they were shivering. The rats chittered their thanks, clambering up onto Jim's shoulders.

'Yes, yes, and the rocks,' Oskar growled.

''Ere, you big tykes,' Maximus the millipede piped up in his tiny voice, 'there's something you all should know—'

Before he could say any more, Oskar pulled Maximus off the window, and swung along the balcony back inside the Lantern Room.

The other animals bundled past Jim as he squinted

at the faraway ship. Maybe the human-people on board could tell him more about his . . . no, *this* was his home.

He jumped through the door in a one-handed twist, landing back inside.

'Please tell me you've finished polishing the lens!'

Claudette ignored him, tapping on the plant pot underneath the on/off switch with her paw. Soil tumbled over, and a mole popped its head out. It scrambled to stand up, glancing blindly around.

'It isn't Thursday again already, is it?' The mole yawned, stretching his pink, stumpy little claw-arms into the air. 'Are you *positive* it's Thursday?'

The cat purred, nudging her face against Norman's, and he nodded, reaching up for the on/off switch.

Jim darted across the Lantern Room, skidding to a halt beside Norman's pot, the Rigging Rats leaping from his shoulder as he knelt next to the mole.

'Hang on! You know you can't turn the beams on with all of us here, Norman, the bulbs will blind us. Wait for us to leave!'

Norman's darkness was the same all day and night, so it was safe for him to stay in the room to turn the bulbs back on, shielding the island from the world's gaze again.

Claudette rubbed her warm, silky fur against Jim's leg, and he scratched her under her chin.

Norman tightened his grip on the on/off switch. 'But it's *Thursday*, Jim,' the mole grumbled. 'We *can't* change the schedule. That would just be,' he shivered, '*unthinkable*. I must do my duty. I *must*. Then get some sleep ready for next week.'

'*Just wait a minute, Norman!*' Oskar yelled.

'It really is . . . mmmpf . . . not a . . . hmmpf . . .' Maximus mumbled inside Oskar's fist.

'Oh, I see where this is going.' Rafi buried his face

in his paws. 'We're all going to be blinded by a blind mole. Such tragic irony!'

Norman pushed the switch up.

'NOOO!' Jim slapped his hands over his eyes as an electric hum surged across the room.

The lighthouse's old, gas-fired lighting gantry hissed and clunked, chugged and juddered. The triple lightbulb frame whirred . . . then coughed like an old man.

All the animals slammed their hands, paws, claws, wings, ears . . . over their eyes.

Maximus's tiny voice insisted, 'I is assurin' you all that you don't need to—'

Jim curled into a ball as the hiss of the gas pumped up inside the bulbs. The clockwork motor below the three bulbs creaked, lurched . . . then the wood-metal frame quivered into life with rubber driving belts spinning and cogs turning. The bulbs rotated on their squeaky-wheeled frame in front of the sea-facing glass, and a pipe sprayed white steam across the Lantern Room.

There was a lot of noise, but no light had seeped through Jim's eyelids. He squinted, then dropped his hands, seeing that none of the animals had their eyes covered now. Because, unthinkably, all the bulbs were still dark.

'Right, see you all next Thursday then,' Norman yawned, crawling back inside his soil mound.

Jim felt dizzy. The beams should be shining across the ocean by now.

Claudette busily licked her paw, lying against Norman's pot, her eyes glinting green. She looked at the bulbs then Jim, before slinking off behind the gantry shaking her head.

Moments like these were when Jim wished Claudette, the Rigging Rats and other animals on the island spoke like him. He knew not all of them wanted to, or could. He'd tried learning their languages, but some were so complicated he couldn't get his voice to make the sounds. It was just lucky for him that, when Edward had been here, many animals had chosen to learn to talk.

'All right, come on . . . it'll be nightfall in eight hours,' he cried, 'and the island has to disappear!'

Tallulah raised her head feathers. 'This is terrible,' she said, flying up near the Espejo lens and landing

28

on Elsa's head. 'Without the projection or beam three-and-a-half . . .'

Jim slammed the on/off lever down, the lighting frame wheezing and shuddering to a stop. 'What's *really* going on here?' He looked at each of the animals. 'Maybe this is a sign?'

Oskar slid his glasses up his nose, squinted at the lantern frame and swung up to look inside the dark bulbs.

Jim hopped from one foot to the other. 'Maybe the bulbs going off is a *sign* that the pirate ship is meant to come to the island?'

Elsa, Tallulah, the Rigging Rats and Rafi all looked at him.

Jim shrugged. 'I'm just thinking . . . you know . . . pirates only steal treasure. And we don't have any treasure on the island, right? So, perhaps we're meant to let them land and help them. Like you did for Edward, all that time ago. And we never get visitors, so I don't get a chance to ask—'

Oskar thudded to the floor in front of Jim, his nostrils flared.

Jim stepped back, swallowing.

'No visitors. That's the end of it,' Oskar grunted.

The wind outside quietened.

'Look, you guys,' Maximus begged, his small voice still muffled by Oskar's fingers, 'if you would just hear me out—'

But Oskar didn't take his eyes off Jim. 'You are older now, but it is *still* our job to keep you safe.'

'So, now it's about stopping this ship reaching our island because you're afraid I'll find out something about myself?'

Oskar grunted. 'It is not like that, no. And this is not just about *you*. It is about protecting us all . . . the whole island.' Oskar looked round at the other animals, pointing up at the lighting gantry. 'Having looked at the lights, there is a far more serious problem. All the filaments inside the bulbs have vanished!'

A long sigh of relief echoed up from Oskar's clenched hand. The orangutan pushed up his glasses in surprise, rolling out his arm, palm and forefinger. 'This little one has been trying to say something for a while, but with the wind outside . . . well, my hearing is not what it was.'

The long, squirming S-shape of the millipede's body

rose up on Oskar's grey ape skin, and Maximus waved his antennae around. 'Tch, just because I'm small it *doesn't* mean you bumwits can all IGNORE ME!'

Jim leant down to Oskar's finger. Maximus sighed again so heavily he felt the millipede's wood-laced breath on his face. 'Look, we *know* how hard you all work in the bug basement, turning our poo into gas to power the lighthouse beams—'

Maximus held up one leg. 'It ain't nothing to do with that. As I've been *trying* to tell you all, we've got one helluva big problem.' The millipede span in a panicky circle on Oskar's palm.

Jim and all the other animals leant in closer, listening.

'As the big ape has deduced . . . someone . . . or *something*,' Maximus gasped, 'has stolen our lightbulb filaments. And I saw them do it!'

CHAPTER FIVE

Oskar curled his hand round, bringing Maximus up to his face. He went cross-eyed behind his little round glasses. 'Do not joke about these strips of tungsten metal, Maximus,' the orangutan snapped. 'You *know* how important they are.'

'Yes, guv'nor, I know,' the millipede tapped a hand (or foot) against the side of his head, 'the bulbs need them for their electric current to pass through, to make light. Without 'em, we have no beams!'

A bead of sweat ran down the side of Oskar's face. Seeing it made Jim's stomach twist into knots.

'Who on the island would steal the filaments? And why?'

Elsa shrugged, Tallulah flap-shrugged and Rafi glanced at the Rigging Rats, all of them puzzled.

Jim curled his arm over his head to scratch it, pacing up and down. He stopped in front of Maximus. 'What did you see? Who was it?'

'Well, as I has been *tryin'* to tell you,' Maximus stomped at least forty-seven legs down on Oskar's palm, 'but no one listens to the *little insect—*'

'Please, Maximus, we only have until sundown.' Jim scrunched up his face to hold back his impatience. 'If you know what happened . . . tell us!'

Maximus cleared his throat, and looked round at his audience. 'It was very dark when I arose early this morning, like I always do.' Maximus crawled to the end of one of Oskar's long, grey fingers. 'And, just as I strolled outside the basement fer some fresh air, I saw a . . . a . . . '

The animals leaned in closer.

'Yes . . . '

Maximus's face turned dark. 'There was a . . . *thing.'*

A collective gulp came from every animal.

'What kind of . . . *thing*?' Rafi blinked. Then blinked some more, his eyes disappearing in the black circles of his raccoon fur. 'If it's bad, I'll stay in bed and you lot can come get me when it's safe.'

33

Tallulah flew around Rafi's head, her bright parrot colours lighting up the room, the grey storm clouds gathering beyond the lighthouse windows. She landed on the raccoon's head, fluffing up her head feathers. 'Rafi, we're trying to listen to Maximus.'

'I sawed a big, dark shadow ... and it crept very quietly *inside* our lighthouse!' Maximus shivered.

The animals drew back, sucking in breaths, and Elsa's trunk swayed sideways, smacking one of the rats, Flum, across the Lantern Room. Flum flew into the stone wall, sliding pancake-like down it before shaking himself off and walking, dizzily, back to the group.

'Sorry, dear,' Elsa cooed. 'I was just shocked someone broke into our home.'

'They didn't break in, Elsa,' Maximus said. 'Someone left the front door open!'

Rafi shook his head. 'I'd never do that. It was probably the cat.'

'No,' Oskar held up his other hand, 'Jim and I were outside on the cliff last night. Late. Listening to Trent and watching the ocean waves.'

Jim looked at Oskar. 'Maybe we didn't close the door properly.'

Maximus leant towards the animals. 'I don't know. But what I *do* know is . . . it was a thing with *HORNS*.' The animals shuffled closer to one another as the wind howled around the lighthouse. 'And spindly legs. It were . . . taller than Elsa!'

'And it crawled inside the lighthouse?' Jim's legs trembled.

'Yes, and there's no way I could 'ave stopped it
. . . with me being so SMALL an' all. And, this *thing,*'
Maximus continued, 'it strolled, bold as brass, into the
lighthouse, as I watched it from the Bug Basement door.
Then, ten minutes later, it bolted out again towards the
orchards!'

Oskar leant over his own hand. 'Then why, *on all the
island's palm trees,* did you not wake us up?'

'Well, guv'nor,' Maximus snapped, a little rattled. 'I
did SHOUT at the time, but you lot were asleep. It's only
us bugs and Claudette up before the crack of dawn.
And, besides, my voice ain't that loud on account of me
bein' so—'

'Small, yes, we got that.' Jim darted to the top of
the Lantern Room's staircase, turning back to look
at the animals and the gantry.

Oskar curled Maximus back inside his hand and
joined Jim. 'We must go after this thief . . . or the island
. . . we . . . I must arrange an all-island meeting to . . .'

Jim put a hand on the orangutan's shoulder. 'Don't
worry, we don't need to panic the whole island.' He
remembered the last time Oskar called one of his
emergency all-island meetings using the broken

36

Narwhal tusk he'd found. Oskar had climbed the rigging of Rum, Flum and Sum's home – a wrecked ship's mast embedded in the island's south beach – and spun the tusk until a *whooom-whooom-whooom* hum filled the air. The sound had whipped through the tusk's middle, rising to a shrill *wheeem-wheeem-wheeem* that echoed out across the island and sea, calling to the animals.

But they didn't have time for all of that. Jim nodded at Oskar. 'I can handle this. I'll take some of the others and we'll set out now. Right, Rafi? I promise, we'll find the thief's tracks, and the filaments!'

Rafi rubbed his stomach. 'Do you think it's possible, before we head off on some foolhardy chase across the island, that we could—'

'Can't go on a mission on an empty stomach, can we? I'll go make breakfast.' Elsa trumpeted a high-pitched note, squeezing her haunches past Jim and back through the Lantern Room staircase door, followed by Oskar and a gleeful Rafi.

Jim paused outside Elsa's room, watching the elephant spin the wooden spokes of an old ship's wheel nailed to the curved wall. Her trunk flicked the wheel round, hard, making it rumble. Elsa's bamboo wood cabinet, stuffed with her bottles of cooking herbs, bowls of dried fruit and napkins folded into swans, shook as the wheel turned.

A deep line appeared in the lighthouse wall, next to the porthole window that Elsa stuck her trunk out of on foggy nights to blow her warning calls across the sea. Then two more lines opened up either side of where Elsa stood, and another split the wall above her head. All of them joined together – four perfectly straight cracks formed a square, spreading wider and wider, a cold breeze rushing into the room, until a huge, elephant-sized door in the lighthouse wall shunted outwards.

Elsa turned to look back at him. 'Are you joining me, deary?'

The large, square slab of thick, solid-stone wall rolled out away from the floor of Elsa's room. Hanging in mid-air for a moment, it grinded upwards, leaving a gaping hole with a high-up view of the ocean stretching to the horizon.

The cold air wrapped around Jim's breeches. He pulled in a breath, before sprinting through the room towards the wall-hole at the same time as Elsa, trumpeting her delight, stepped off her bedroom floor and out into nothingness.

CHAPTER SIX

The blast of freezing air hit Jim as he leapt past Elsa, out of the square hole and into the void. Heart in his throat, he dropped down beside the outside wall of the lighthouse.

Hundreds of smooth, stone slats, all slanted downwards and jutting out around the outside wall in a gentle curve, flicked Jim's legs up when he landed on them. Skimming over the slats suspended hundreds of feet in the air, he laughed as he helter-skeltered around the lighthouse. Shooting downwards, the slats were grinding out of the lighthouse wall seconds before he slid over them.

Elsa zipped down the lighthouse slide's curve after him, her huge stumpy elephant legs flailing around. As he flew off the slide's end, Jim flung his arms in the

air, whooping with joy . . .

. . . before eating a mouthful of hay.

Spitting it out, he rolled off the hay pile at the bottom of the slide, just before Elsa flopped into it next to him. She leapt to her feet, shaking her trunk side to side, the stone slats behind her shunting back inside the lighthouse walls. Jim ran after the animals spilling out of the lighthouse front door, while Elsa headed inside to the kitchen, and he caught up with them at the outhouse, watching Oskar swing up on to the stone building's roof.

The orangutan held Maximus up to the sky, his hand silhouetted in the morning sun. 'Which way did this horned thing go?'

'Ah, um . . .' The millipede scratched his head with six legs. 'Lift me higher, would you, guv'nor?' The millipede squinted across the sea, up at the distant northern Charcoal Tree, the orchards, and the valley beyond the Thistle Meadows, leading to the island's far eastern edge and the Craggy Caves. 'Hmm, yes, it went through the thistles.'

Oskar leapt to the edge of the roof and looked down at Jim and the other animals. 'The horned thief escaped across the island,' he grunted, jabbing a finger at the skyline. 'Our filaments lie that way.'

'Um, but we don't have to go after them . . . *right* now, do we?' Rafi winced his whiskers. 'Only, I'm *ever so* hungry. Did I say "ever so"? I meant *ridiculously* hungry.'

Rum, Flum and Sum chittered, rubbing their rat bellies, and Jim scooped the three of them up into a hug, scratching each of their chins in turn.

Tallulah *clack-clocked* her beak together, licking it with her grey tongue and bobbing her head up and down. 'Yes, food!'

'All right.' Jim gave in. 'None of us have had breakfast yet. We'll eat, *then* set off. But this is serious . . . we have to get our filaments back before nightfall to stop that pirate ship or—'

A cloud of dust sprayed into Jim's face as all the animals bolted back to the lighthouse.

He brushed himself down and ran across the rocky lawn to a long table crammed with food Elsa had brought out. There were bowls of chopped mango, watermelon and banana, mounds of yellow cheese, huge loaves of crusty bread, juicy cacti segments, apple pies, jugs of custard, piles of cabbage leaves, a pyramid of peaches and almonds, palm leaves with mussels and limpets scattered on them, and bucketloads of orange juice.

'You'll need full stomachs to go after this thief,' Elsa said, smiling from big ear to big ear.

Oskar took Jim's hand in his. 'You will not know it, Jim, but today is a special day.'

'Can we eat yet? I'm *ludicrously* starving!' Rafi

reached across to the trash-can lid on the table in front of him.

Oskar glared at the raccoon.

'As I was saying,' Oskar turned to Jim, 'today, it is exactly twelve years since you landed on our island.' The orangutan pulled a leather pouch out from behind his back. 'You came from beyond and, alongside us, became a lighthouse keeper. You have worked hard, you have learnt well . . . you have found a place in our family.' Oskar's voice broke and he wiped away a tear, holding out the pouch to Jim. 'This is a small gift from us all.'

Jim's cheeks rushed with heat as he looked down at the bumpy pouch. The sharp tang of its leather filled his nostrils.

'Thank you,' he said, clearing his throat. To be given any gift by the animals was a special treat.

'Open it, open it!' cawed Tallulah.

Jim flicked the pouch open and bright silver glinted in the sunshine. It was jam-packed with hand-crafted tools, and Jim gently pulled a steel claw hammer from its slot. Grabbing the smooth, wooden handle, he swung the hammer up and down. It felt heavy. Solid.

There were three different-sized screwdrivers, an adjustable spanner, wood saw, scraper, wire cutters, pliers, ruler and pencil in the pouch too.

Ever since he could remember, Jim had helped Oskar around the lighthouse. There were always rusty bolts in the Lantern Room to oil, shelves to be built in the animals' rooms, steam-powered ploughs to repair for farming, coconut shell cocoon homes to be hammered together for the butterfly larvae down in the bug basement, and Oskar's outhouse – which *always* smelt of bananas and sweet potatoes – was a magical, higgledy-piggledy workshop strewn with half-built inventions.

Jim had learnt so much from Oskar, and he hoped one day to be as skilled at soldering, screwing, sawing and carving.

Jim looked up at Oskar, a lump in his throat. 'You made all this for me? You're . . . so clever.'

The orangutan stepped forward, pulling the pouch out of Jim's hands and unravelling two long, thin strips of leather from each of its ends. 'See, it is a belt too.' An excited sparkle shone in Oskar's voice. 'You can take it with you wherever you go.' The orangutan fastened the straps around Jim's waist, clipping them together with a shiny buckle.

Jim tipped the pouch to see how it looked, and he tingled all over. 'Oh . . . my . . . I don't know what to . . . I *love it*!' The weight of the tools felt good. Like . . . something he *needed* to wear. 'You have gone to so much trouble to—'

'*Jeeez*, can we eat yet? I . . . am . . . *exceedingly starving*!' Rafi rummaged his tiny paws around in the old lettuce leaves, carrots and fish bones on his trash-can lid.

Oskar shot Rafi another look, but Jim rubbed the orangutan's shoulder, leaning towards the animals and smiling. 'LET'S EAT!'

CHAPTER SEVEN

Elsa trumpeted her delight, thumping to the ground to join the others around the table. She grabbed an apricot tree branch with her trunk, stripping bark from it, as her ear knocked Claudette sideways. The cat took no notice and sniffed at some soya beans. She turned her nose up, devouring some mussels instead.

Cornelius scuttled along the table, sucking up wet lumps of green algae, his eye-stalks watching the Rigging Rats scamper up and down. Jim threw tiny chunks of cheese at the rats, which they always caught then nibbled on. Maximus wriggled over a lump of rotten wood, licking his lips, and Tallulah swooped down past Oskar – in a blaze of parrot yellows, reds and greens – to snatch a piece of pineapple out of the orangutan's fingers, *ca-cawing* with laughter as Oskar

bit the end of his empty fingers.

Jim scoffed three peaches, two bowls of custard and twelve lumps of cheese, laughing as Tallulah dive-bombed back and forth across the table.

'Eat your own food, Tallulah!' Elsa yelled as the parrot snapped an apricot from her branch on the way past and then flew up to the top of the lighthouse.

'So . . .' Jim chomped on a strawberry and turned

to Oskar. 'What do we do if we can't find this horned beast thief thing?'

The orangutan's expression darkened. 'You must. The island and everything that lives here depends on it.'

Jim gulped down the strawberry, watching the animals stuffing their faces. The table was scattered with fruit pips, juice stains and empty shells. But with the storm clouds in the distance, they couldn't sit here much longer. He shoved his chair back and stood up.

'Thank you, Elsa, for such a—'

SPLAT!

A yellow, lumpy slop of custard hit his forehead, ran down his eyelids, over his cheeks and into his nostrils. A gloopy dollop dribbled into his mouth . . . and he licked it away, spying Rafi doubled over, chuckling. Jim narrowed his eyes, pausing, then leant across the table, grabbed a handful of mango slices, squeezed them in his hand, and threw the orange slush at Rafi.

SPLOSH-SPLAT!

The raccoon's black and white face-fur was slapped with mango mush, bubbling and farting as it tumbled down his jowls. '*FOOD FI—*'

Blurry, hurricane-force streams of hay, cheese, squashed bananas, grapes, bread, cake, algae, slabs of bark and slimy custard clumps flew across the table.

In seconds, every animal and boy was a dribbling mess of bright green, orange, yellow, and red chunky, snot-like food rivers that dripped down their fur, feathers, hides, hairs and skin.

Elsa blew lumps of algae at Cornelius from her trunk, the crab flying off the table with a *paaaarp*. Rafi smeared peaches into Flum and Sum's feet, so they rolled about with their new giant, wrinkly bunions. Jim jammed a slab of pineapple on the end of Tallulah's curved beak as she swooped back down to the table, the parrot flicking her head left and right, and Claudette batted limpet after limpet at Oskar's head with her tail as—

Oskar held his arm up.

The table went quiet.

Sssh-splat.

The pineapple slid off Tallulah's beak, landing on Maximus. The millipede wriggled out from underneath it.

Cornelius flicked a lump of straggly brown seaweed

at Jim's head. 'Oh,' the crab peered round at everyone, 'have we finished?'

The seaweed slid down Jim's nose, dropping to the ground with a quiet *plop*.

'Tungsten,' Oskar grunted, all eyes staring at him, whilst blinking away bits of food. The orangutan picked custard-coated straw off his face with a stern expression. 'Tungsten is a rare and strong metal. It can withstand huge amounts of heat without melting, and it is *essential* for beam three-and-a-half to warm up the ring of light-bending seawater around the island to create the illusion that we have disappeared. So, this thief—'

'Horned beast thief—'

'Yes, thank you, Maximus. This horned beast thief stole our precious tungsten and we must get it back.'

AARF-AARF-AARF!

The seals down on Seal Cove beach began bellowing a chorus of deafening cries. What had upset them? Jim jumped up, running across the field and past the lighthouse's north side to the cliff edge. With half-chewed bits of food and slopping custard trailing behind them, the animals followed, lining up alongside him, staring wide-eyed down into the cove.

AARF-AARF-AARF!

Along the curve of beach below, bobbing up and down with every wave, were hundreds of pieces of . . . what were they? Big, small, long and short, it looked like splinters of wood were floating in the sea.

All the seals down on the sand had thrust their heads up in the air, barking their distress.

Jim's throat went bone dry.

CHAPTER EIGHT

Oskar vaulted across the cliff-side grass and tapped Claudette on her shoulder. She meowed, but didn't take her eyes off the spectacle below.

'Do you know what time the lighthouse beams went off, Claudette?' The orangutan pushed his glasses up his grey button nose as Claudette looked up at him. 'If the water mirage around us has been down, you must tell me how long the island has been visible.'

The cat hissed at him, and ran off towards the lighthouse.

Oskar rubbed his forehead, glancing down at the expanse of floating debris. 'That cat, she is . . .'

'Complicated? And, by the looks of things, definitely not going on the tungsten mission,' Elsa finished.

'Nor are we, we are too old!' Oskar said.

'Speak for yourself, dear,' Elsa smiled. 'But, come to think about it, I *could* already do with a cup of tea after all this excitement.'

'All cats are moody about *something*. It's that look in their—'

'All right, Rafi.' Jim crouched next to the raccoon. 'You know Claudette takes her duty very seriously. Maybe she's upset about the bulbs, like we are.'

'She may be feeling guilty?' Elsa said. 'Perhaps she tried to stop the thief . . . but couldn't. And she knows what losing the beams means to the island.'

Oskar paced up and down, jabbing a long finger down at Seal Cove. 'This is terrible!'

Heart thumping in his chest, Jim lowered himself down past the cliff's grass-line, scraping his bottom across the dirt. He squinted down at the dark flotsam in the water. 'Those fragments might be clues to who or what the thief is.'

'Wait!' Oskar knelt beside him and Jim stopped. 'You *know* the rules. It is the seals' beach and they *hate* us going down there. We must respect that.'

'But we have tungsten to find and pirates to turn away. There *are* no rules right now!' Jim dropped down, scrambling over loose shingle. He looked back up at Oskar. 'Don't worry, I'll be quick.'

Jim leapt down the cliff, grabbing clumps of grass as he went. Rolling over a ledge, he slid down the steep slope of soil, shingle and dead trees. Waving up at the line of animal silhouettes, he saw Oskar scanning the ocean with his spyglass.

Jim skidded over a large, slippery rock and then . . .

crunch, his feet landed on the beach shingle. Ahead, was an endless span of grey-brown bumps – hundreds of wriggling, growling, *aarfing* blubber mounds.

They all looked up at Jim.

He gulped.

Stepping forward, the shingle crunching loudly, he reached the first wall of mottled grey flab. The seal's whiskery scrunched-up nose sniffed the air as he got closer, and it swivelled fourteen chins round to look at him.

The animal's eyes were big, brown pools of sadness. Jim half-smiled, but the seal just stared back, unmoving, a rim of watery tears brimming in its eyes.

All the seals had sad eyes; when trouble came to their beach, they felt it deeply.

Jim shimmied past the first seal and carefully moved onwards through the narrow blubber-gaps between seals. Most ignored him, their *aarfing* barks calming now, some grunted and shuffled their wobbly bodies away from him as he slipped past.

Near the water's edge, he wriggled between two last lumps and waded into the freezing water, drenching his cloth shoes and breeches. Leaping through the waves, he realised that what had looked like broken bits of wood from up on the cliff, wasn't that at all. Jim scooped up some of the slimy yellow-brown material bobbing around him. These strands of debris floating on the water were . . . *paper*.

Glancing along the beach, hundreds of torn, soaked pieces of parchment clogged up the shoreline.

Jim threw the dripping paper aside, surging left and right through the water, picking up slops of parchment, one after another, trying to read them; some fell apart as he lifted them out of the water, others coiled together like drenched cotton. Wading along the shoreline, he scanned for any pieces that were intact.

Just ahead, rising over the curve of a wave, was a full square of paper, floating printed-side up, the ink looking like it hadn't smeared in the sea. He dived into the water, swimming to the parchment—

The paper exploded up into the air, a huge gush of water followed by a vanilla-coloured seal's head.

Jim flailed to a stop in the water, and the seal growled at him, wet strands of the now-ripped parchment sliding off its nose and into the sea. *Pfffssssttttt.* The seal sprayed a warm jet of stinking, fishy water out its mouth, hitting Jim in the face.

Spitting the water out, he frantically wiped his face, coughing and spluttering.

'Young man,' the seal declared in a matriarchal tone, whilst scraping the remaining parchment off her nose with a flipper. 'You are *intruding* on *our* beach. I suggest you retreat back to *your* part of the island. Forthwith.'

Pulling a fishbone out of his nostril, Jim heaved. 'I really think you should clean your teeth.'

The seal snorted. 'Did you hear what I said?'

'Yes, I heard you!' Jim waded back to the shore, huffing. 'I just wanted to read what was on these parchments. That's *all.*'

The seal *aarfed* and lifted her body into the air, clapping her front flippers together. Immediately, thirty other seals body-slammed across the shingle, forming a huge semi-circle around Jim.

The vanilla-coloured seal slid out of the sea and waddled up to Jim, raising her plump body so they were nose-to-nose. Opening her mouth, she breathed into Jim's face.

Retching as the sour, putrid blast of rotten fish wafted over his skin, Jim closed his eyes for a moment.

'You did that on purpose!'

The seal smirked.

Jim glanced round at the other seals – hundreds of sad, black eyes brightened as they all clapped their flippers and opened their whiskery mouths to *aarf-aarf-aarf* at him.

'Come on, it *was* quite funny,' the vanilla-coloured seal said, slapping Jim on the shoulder. He half-smiled as the matriarch whistled and all the seals instantly stopped their guffaws. 'However, this *is* our beach, and you *should* leave.' The seal bent down and scooped up a section of parchment lying nearby. She passed it to Jim on her flipper. 'These floated here from over yonder. It is what you came for, now you can go.'

Jim took the soggy, fragile piece of paper and looked at it. Some of the ink had run, and parts of the paper were torn, but what was left, read:

WANTED

Safe return of this ~~Baby~~ Boy.
To Ocracoke, North Carolina.

'T'were lost
at sea near
Nassau,
the Year
of Our
Lord 1704.

REWARD

A King's ~~Ransom~~ of Treasure

If My ~~Boy~~ is harmed,
You'll be ~~fed to the sharks!~~

CHAPTER NINE

Jim's stomach flipped as he read the blotched parchment again. He looked up at the vanilla-coloured seal, heart thumping in his throat. 'Did . . . these come from that ship heading towards the island?' He glanced out to sea at the faraway silhouette of the pirate ship, easily still a day's sailing away.

The vanilla-coloured seal shrugged. 'When the light beams were off last night, we found it unsettling. So we swam out farther for fish, under the cover of darkness, and bumped into that ship's anchor. Many of us are curious,' the seal matriarch looked round at the crowd, '*and* stupid, so we poked our noses up because crews on these vessels sometimes throw food scraps overboard. And, well, we're lazy hunters.' A few *oorf-oorfs* rose up from the seal crowd. 'But there were no scraps. Just *those* . . . flying off the ship in the wind.' The seal sighed. 'Now, young man, they're clogging up our cove. Sailors are strange creatures . . .'

Jim shoved the parchment into his breeches and ran back across the beach. He spun around, waving at the vanilla-coloured seal as he ran. 'Thanks for your help!'

The seal shook her head. '*Boys* are strange creatures,' she muttered, glancing at the other seals. They stared at her expectantly. She raised her head and opened her whiskery jaw wide, yelling after Jim: '*And don't come back to our beach again!*'

The colony *aarf-aarf-aarfed* as one, clapping their flippers as Jim clambered back to the base of the cliff.

Whumpf.

A rope hit the soil next to him.

Looking up, Elsa's trunk was dangling over the cliff edge, the rope's other end spun round her tusks. Jim tied the rope around his waist and . . . was standing back up at the clifftop in the blink of an elephant's eye.

'Miserable bunch those seals, aren't they?' Rafi said, the animals gathering around Jim.

Ignoring the raccoon, Jim held up the torn, wet parchment. 'They're looking for *me*!' He tapped his finger on the paper's smudged sketch of a baby in a barrel of rum. 'That ship's here for me and this *king's treasure*!' He glanced at Oskar, breathing fast, as he showed the parchment to the orangutan. 'You said there *was* no treasure on the island, but maybe those pirates are coming to—'

Oskar held up his hand. 'The treasure is the reward for you. It is not here on the island, I assure you. But perhaps those pirates do not know that. Either way, we must stop that ship reaching us . . . and you.' Oskar walked away towards the lighthouse.

Pushing Rafi aside, Jim ran after Oskar, waving the tatty paper at him. 'You know who wrote this, don't you!'

Oskar stopped and stamped his foot. Breathing in, he turned to Jim, his beady eyes watery behind his glasses.

Jim swallowed. 'You *do* know who my parents are.'

'Enough!' Oskar snapped. Elsa and the other animals were crowding behind him, looking at Jim. 'There is no time to explain! I am sorry, Jim. It will all

63

have to wait. There is a storm coming, and we must get the lighthouse lanterns back on. It is our duty as lighthouse keepers to stop ships finding us, and stop them crashing into Black Eel Rock!'

Jim stared at Oskar.

Oskar stared back. With one long arm, he beckoned the other animals. 'Come on, no more dilly-dallying. We have a thief to catch and our bulb filaments to find!'

Jim watched the animals leave his side as a gust of wind swept over the cliff. He shivered, slamming a hand on his tricorn hat to stop it blowing away.

In the distance, the pirate ship was getting closer.

Looking at the ink-stained parchment, he felt dizzy. They needed to get the lighthouse beams working again, and he had to go on that mission. He just wasn't sure, now he knew they were looking for him, if he *wanted* to turn that ship away any more.

Oskar watched Jim and a group of the animals disappear through the orchards and into the distance, where the thistle meadows began. Pushing his glasses up his nose, he sighed.

Curling her trunk round as she squeezed out of the

lighthouse door, Elsa laid a tray of tea and biscuits on the – very messy – breakfast table.

Oskar looked at her. 'Have I done the right thing?'

Elsa sat down next to him and picked up the china teapot, pouring them both a cup of tea.

'We all knew this day would come, my dear.' Elsa deftly picked up a teaspoon with the curled tip of her trunk, adding some sugar before stirring her tea.

'The others are with him.'

'But if he finds out all that we know, he may want to—'

'Drink some tea, deary.' Elsa lifted her cup out of its saucer, spun it round and delicately tipped some tea into her giant mouth. 'We've sheltered him from the truth thus far, but now he's almost old enough to make his own choices.'

Oskar slammed his teacup down. 'But, Elsa, he has no idea how bad his people can be!'

The elephant poured more tea. 'Children are impossible sometimes, my dear. But you have to let them find their own way.' Elsa sucked five biscuits up her trunk, swallowing them whole. 'Wrapping them in cotton wool can make things worse.'

Oskar nodded. 'You are right. As usual. But something is coming, Elsa. Something bad. I can feel it.'

'That may be so, but for now let's just get on with our work around here.' Elsa gathered up the flowery tea set and stood up. 'Jim and the others will be back in no time . . . with the tungsten. I have no doubt.'

Oskar's expression went dark. 'Yes, but what if he finds out that . . . ?'

But Elsa was already shuffling back through the lighthouse door.

Oskar leant down to pick up the Charleville rifle, laying it across his lap. Staring out at the ocean's horizon, he unfolded the old note he'd brought from his room.

To Whomsoever,

It is my ardent hope that you have found my boy alive and well.

I know what you will think of me – abandoning him, a baby, to the sea in a barrel of rum – but I do love him. And it is because I love him that I'm sending him away from me. Away from the danger I face every day. Away from the dark force he, too, would have battled if he had stayed with me.

So, whoever you are, please take care of my son. Teach him well. Let him be himself. And love him as much as I do.

Yours,

Mary

Oskar watched the pirate ship sailing closer, tears welling in his eyes.

CHAPTER TEN

Scrambling through the soil seed troughs at the far edges of the lighthouse farmyard garden were the Rigging Rats. Chittering to one another, they ran at full pelt through cabbages, lettuce patches and potato fields, pushing each other over at any opportunity. Jim ran alongside Rum as the rat jumped on Flum's head and over Sum, with Tallulah flying in circles above and Rafi huffing and puffing behind them.

Jim slowed down, turning to Maximus on his shoulder as the millipede's legs rippled in the slip-stream. 'Which way did you say the thief went?'

'He . . . she . . . *IT* . . . ran towards those thistles, Jim,' yelled Maximus, into his ear.

Jim swerved south, away from the black, jagged outline of the lightning-struck Charcoal Tree to the island's north, and towards the rough, thorny border of the island's Thistle Meadows.

When he got there, he skidded to a stop. The thistles were taller than him, like a wall of spiky trees.

'If I were a thief,' he said, 'I'd go in there, because no one would go after me.'

'Except us!' Tallulah squawked above. 'Although, admittedly, I can fly over the thistles.'

Rafi bumped into Jim's legs, both of them stumbling forward. 'Why did you stop, Jim . . . ah, I see. Wow. That's a lot of thorns. Probably too many. Let's turn back.' The raccoon started walking away.

Jim grabbed Rafi's paw, pulling him back round in a circle to the thistles. 'No, Rafi, we have a mission to finish.'

The raccoon groaned. 'I won't have any fur left by the time we come out the other side!'

'Rafi has a point,' Maximus said, bobbing up and down on Jim's shoulder. 'Should we find a way around?'

Jim shook his head. 'What if the thief is *hiding* in the thistles?'

'Well, let's at *least* eat before we go any farther, we've come miles and I'm starving.'

Tallulah flapped down onto the raccoon's head. 'Rafi, you have run precisely two minutes, forty-three seconds across one field.'

Rafi looked back at the lighthouse. 'Right. Yes. I knew that.' His stomach made a long, growling sound.

The nearest thistle plant had inch-long spikes on its stem, and a huge blue-purple bauble of spines at its tip.

'I can get us through this,' Jim said and, with a *sssssshhhhhiiiinnnnngggggg,* unsheathed the rusted-silver curved sword from his bedroom wall.

Tallulah, Rum, Flum and Sum, Rafi and Maximus's eyes all widened.

'Are you even old enough to have that?' Tallulah cawed, scrambling behind Rafi's ear to hide.

Swiiish-swiish. Jim swiped the cutlass back and forth, remembering Oskar telling him it had washed-up on the island with Edward. 'I know what I'm doing!' he said nervously, hacking at the nearest thistle plant.

He missed, spun in two full circles – slicing a chunk of black-grey hair off Rafi's head – and fell to the ground.

'Aaah!' Rafi patted his head with his tiny front paws. *'What have you done?* How will I ever get a girlfriend now?'

Tallulah cawed, flying up behind Rafi's ear. 'Your face is still the same, so *that* won't help either.'

Rafi glared at her.

'I'm so sorry, Rafi!' Jim said as the raccoon gathered up bits of his hair, licked it and stuck it back on his head. All of it fell off again.

Jim sighed. This was a *great* start to the mission.

'Maybe I can't do this.' Jim picked himself and the

sword back up, holding it gingerly.

'You CAN,' Maximus insisted next to Jim's earlobe. 'Just aim the cutlass at the plants you wanna cut!'

Rum, Flum and Sum nodded frantically at Jim.

Trying to remember what Oskar had taught him, Jim sliced the cutlass low and sideways.

Three thistle plants collapsed.

'Yes!'

He hacked down two more plants, their purple crowns toppling, then kept chopping. In no time, an opening appeared, and soon there was a small, windy path through the thistles, big enough for him and the animals to clamber along.

They all ducked under the taller plants that had fallen together in jagged arches, needles scraping Jim's head as the brush got thicker and blocked out the sunlight.

Mud squished through his cloth shoes and up between his toes.

'These thistle things eventually come to an end, right?' Rafi swiped a thorny stalk out of his face whilst, by Jim's feet, the Rigging Rats were happily padding their way across the bog, barely noticing the thistles.

'Just,' Jim swiped five thistle plants down, 'keep,' and brought the cutlass up to attack another three, '*going*!'

As these last three thistles fell, the plants thinned out, making it easier to crawl in between spiky stumps without getting stabbed or scraped. Jim jumped over a log lying across the path, sliding to a muddy stop in front of a large bright green pond. The others joined him, all looking across the slimy water, lilies floating on its surface and a big brown knobbly rock in its middle.

Rafi grimaced, holding his nose. 'This place *stinks*.'

'Whoa, *that's* saying something coming from your seven-year unwashed self,' Tallulah said, landing on Rafi's head.

Jim dropped the cutlass and knelt down next to the pond. Sweating from his thistle-slaying effort, he went to dip his hands in the cool pond water to splash his face.

'I wouldn't, Jim,' Maximus warned. 'This 'ere water is bad.'

The millipede was right – the pond water had a thick odour of stale cheese, garlic farts and rotten onions. Jim stood up and looked around. The thistles thinned out in all directions as if afraid to go near the water.

He pointed to the far side of the pond. 'Look, a bridge!' A tree trunk, carved flat and laid across the left edge, floated on the surface-slime. 'We should cross there.'

'Yes, let's. Honestly, this place smells worse than Cornelius's parps!' Rafi twitched his nose at the same time as the knobbly brown rock in the middle of the pond flicked open two huge eyes.

Jim and the Rigging Rats jumped back.

The knobbly brown rock yawned a wide mouth out of the dark pond water.

'YAAAAAR-RIIIBBBETT!' the rock croaked.

Rafi's fur snapped upright as he leapt into the air and turned round to face the rock's huge mouth. Gulping, the raccoon backed up into Jim.

'Greet-a-macheekas!' the rock yelled. 'What you guys do-a-looing at my pond?'

Jim swallowed. 'You're not a rock. You're a . . . very big frog.'

The knobbly brown rock-frog rolled his eyes.

'Wrong. Stoopid-ee-do-doopeedee two-legged weirdo. Me a *toad*!'

'Right, sorry.' Jim picked up his cutlass and sheathed it. 'We, um, didn't mean to disturb you. We're just on our way through to catch a—'

Rafi slammed his arm across Jim's chest. 'Don't,' he hissed, leaning in to whisper, 'how do we know *he* isn't the thief?'

'Feef? What one of those?' The toad slithered his huge, knobbly body forwards.

Ripples of slime slapped out of the pond and over Jim's feet; he closed his eyes, shivering, as the gunk slid down between his toes.

'Is feef like cheese? Me Toad . . . me like cheese-a-reese. You weirdos got cheese?'

Jim glanced round at Rafi, raising an eyebrow.

'Yeah, OK,' said Rafi. 'He isn't the thief.'

Jim rummaged inside the satchel of food Elsa had given them, pulling out three chunks of cheese.

The knobbly toad's eyes widened to the size of dinner plates. 'Cheeeeeese! You weirdos bring Toad cheese-a-reese! Me like you guys.'

Jim held out the cheese, then drew it back. 'Hang

75

on, these are our rations for our journey . . . why am I giving them to a frog?'

'TOAD!' Maximus yelled from his shoulder.

'Yes, *toad* . . . what will you give us in exchange for the cheese?'

The knobbly toad licked his slimy lips. 'A big kiss?'

Rum, Flum and Sum bent over, miming being sick.

Jim narrowed his eyes. 'Something sensible!'

The toad glanced around. 'Me let you . . . cross da bridge?'

Rafi rolled his eyes. 'Wow, I *never* guessed he was going to say that.'

Jim scratched his head and looked at the tree trunk floating on the pond water. 'That's not good enough. You need to offer us more.'

Tallulah flapped over and landed on Jim's head, ruffling out her red, green and yellow chest feathers. 'Yes, toad. We need *information* about a thief.'

'Da feef. Tell me, what is dis? S'like a skin problem or sumfink?' The toad rubbed his knobbly chin with a webbed foot. 'Dafeef. *Da-feef.* Can you catch it from sitting in a slimy pond all day?'

Rafi smacked his face into his paws, sighing.

Jim took a deep breath. 'Let's start at the beginning, shall we? What . . . is . . . your . . . name, toad?' He stepped forward, leant over the pond and patted the toad's slimy, knobbly brown skin.

The toad closed his eyes. For a long time.

'Toad!' the toad finally yelped, licking his long, wide lips. He looked at the cheese in Jim's hand and swished his bulky body up and down in the pond slime, slapping the putrid water around excitedly. 'Yep-a-ma-pep! Me Toad. Me love pond, cheese and butterflies.'

Jim laughed. He'd lived on this island all his life and had never ventured inside the Thistle Meadows, so had never known a giant toad, called Toad, lived here.

'Um, Mr Toad—'

'Me Toad, not Mr Toad.'

'Right, yes, sorry,' Jim flicked slime off one of his wet feet. 'Toad, we're on an important mission. You see, da feef . . . I mean, *the thief* . . . has stolen some special metal from inside our lighthouse bulbs.'

'Da naughty feefy.'

'Exactly. So naughty that if we don't find the feef

. . . *thief* . . . and the metal they took,' Jim took a breath, 'then the island's lighthouse won't be able to light up the sea, sending out a shimmery mirage to hide us *or* stop ships from getting wrecked on the rocks.'

'Whoa. Your life comply-womply-cated. Me Toad in pond, with cheese and butterflies. Very happy.' Toad spread his knobbly, brown lips into a wide grin.

'Yes, I can see that.' Toad's beaming grin was so joyful Jim couldn't stop himself smiling back. 'So, as you spend a lot of time in your pond . . . if we gave you all of this cheese, would you remember if you've seen a thief running over your bridge?'

'Hey, hang on a minute . . . give him *all* the cheese? I'd like some—'

'Sssh, Rafi.' Jim lifted a finger up to his lips.

Rafi sighed, staring lovingly at the chunks of cheese in Jim's palm.

'Did da feef have big horns?' Toad asked.

'Yes!' Jim, Rafi, Maximus and Tallulah yelled.

The Rigging Rats chittered excitedly too.

'Did da feef run dis way at darkly-sparkly night?'

'Yes!' they all bellowed together.

'Did da feef have fwree teeny-tiny bits of

78

sheeny-shiny metal it were carrying?' The toad's eyes were wide and a little ecstatic at this question.

'YES!' the group shouted.

Toad rubbed his knobbly chin in thought. 'Nope, sorry. Ain't seen dis da feef.'

Jim and the others groaned.

Toad slapped the slimy pond water – sending it flying across all of them – as he guffawed loudly. '*Hur-hur*. Toad make joke! *Hur-hur*. Course I seen da feef, you weirdos!'

Rafi growled through clenched teeth, whilst Maximus flipped in a relieved circle on Jim's shoulder.

'Very . . . *very* funny,' Jim said. 'When did you—'

'Ooooh-oh . . . a wickle-pickle caty-pillar!' Toad yelled, noticing Maximus for the first time, his webbed feet splashing slime-water over the pond's edge. Toad clambered heavily towards Jim. 'Oooh, I *love* me caty-pillars. Dey turn into boot-ee-ful butterflies! Me talk loveliness wiv butterflies, so can me talk loveliness wiv—'

'I'm a *millipede*,' Maximus said.

Toad frowned and cocked his big, knobbly head to one side at Maximus. 'What, so no pretty-flitty wings?

No lovey-dovey talking?'

Maximus shook his head. 'No. Sorry.'

Toad pulled his foot back inside the pond, huffing. He rippled his lips up and down on the water, green, slimy bubbles spreading across the pond, rising up like popping frogspawn. 'Okay den, millipede.'

'You've seen this thief, then?' Maximus leant forward on Jim's shoulder.

'Fing is,' Toad replied, 'me spend a lot-a-lotta time sleeping in dis pond. Don't see everyone who runs along Toad's bridge. Shame cos Toad likes to chat with weirdos like you weirdos.' Toad considered his own words. 'But, luckily, da thought of cheese-a-reese in Toad's tummy has made me 'member about da feef.'

80

Jim raised his eyebrows, spinning his hand at Toad. 'Yes, and . . .'

'Da feef ran past Toad's pond at moon-time, 1.32 a.m. It was big, fat and was carrying fwree strips of tungsten in its mouth.' Toad nodded.

Rafi turned to Jim, wide-eyed. 'Did we tell him the lightbulb metal was tungsten?'

Jim shook his head.

'Toad cleverererer than he look-a-mook!' Toad grinned.

'And where was the thief going with our tungsten?' demanded Jim.

'Well . . . funny you ask . . . cos all da tiny cutey-wootey creatures whispered to Toad that da feef runned towards da Craggy Caves,' announced Toad. 'Cheese now.'

Jim stepped up onto the bridge, holding out the cheese. 'How can I get the cheese to you—'

WHIZZ-FLICK-SHLURP-SLAP!

'Eewwww! Oh . . . pleeease no! That . . . was . . . DIS-GUS-TING!' Jim flicked Toad's yellow saliva off his hand and arm, wiping them across a nearby rock. He looked down to see his body soaked in yellow toad

81

tongue slime.

'Hmm, yum-yum-yum cheeeeese!' Toad hummed, gulping the last bit down. 'Toad now happy-as-lappy for days. Thankoo!'

'MMMPFF!' came a muffled cry seemingly from inside Jim's brain. *'NNNMMMPFFF!'*

Jim stuck a finger in his ear and dug around. Tiny, slime-covered feet grabbed his finger and, with a faint *pop*, he pulled Maximus out of his earhole, gently wiping the toad-spit off the horrified millipede.

Jim trotted across the bridge, followed by Rafi and the Rigging Rats. 'I think it's time to get going. Thanks for your help, Toad!'

'Yep-a-la-mep . . . now go, go, go to da caves under da Barnacle Blowhole. Byse-y-bye, weirdos!' Toad closed his eyes and sank back down into his pond, once again a knobbly, brown rock. 'RIIIBBETT!'

CHAPTER ELEVEN

After another hour of hacking their way through the giant thistles, they stumbled out into the sunshine. Huffing and puffing, Jim leant on his shaking knees, catching his breath. He slid his cutlass back inside its scabbard as Maximus crawled to the far side of his shoulder.

They found themselves at the top of a wide hill. Spread out below them was a narrow, U-shaped valley covered in a sloping carpet of red, orange and yellow flowers waving side to side in the pre-storm breeze.

'Eagle Valley,' Rafi whispered.

The two hills on either side of the valley swept upwards into ragged crests of rocks at their peaks. Covered in streams of yellow moss, flowing down their edges like custard, the rock formations curled

out over the valley floor, creating two massive, jutting ledges. The curved ledges were sharp and had nothing holding them up as they spanned out across the valley. Almost meeting in the middle, it seemed impossible – looking at them from this far away – that the two half-circle ledges stayed up in the air.

'Beaks,' Jim said.

'Bless you,' Tallulah cawed, swirling around the group.

'No, I said *beaks*,' Jim repeated. 'They look like two eagles trying to bite each other from either side of the valley—'

'SSSSSSH!' Maximus yelled. 'They'll blimmin' hear us.'

Rafi swallowed, hard.

Jim did too.

Three little gulps came from Rum, Flum and Sum, and Jim crouched down to stroke each of the rats' heads in turn.

'The thief must have come this way to get to the blowhole,' Jim said. 'The Craggy Caves are on the other side of the valley.'

'You do know you will have to run for this part.'

Tallulah's voice was very timid as she flapped down on to Jim's head. 'And I mean *run fast* . . . from the eagles.'

Jim took a deep breath, lifting a hand up to rub Tallulah's red-green belly feathers. She head-bumped his fingers.

'My legs are only little,' Rafi informed everyone. 'And you gave that toad all *my* cheese, so I have no energy left for running.'

Jim chuckled and gently tweaked one of Rafi's ears. 'If I told you there was a mountain of rotten cabbage, orange peel and half-chewed apples on the other side of this valley, Rafi, you'd run.'

'*What?* Is there? Shall we get going right now . . . oh, I see, you were making a point. *Tch.*' Rafi shook Jim's hand off, huffing. 'Are we *sure* we have to do this?'

The raccoon gazed across the valley, a gust of wind forcing the grass down into a giant swaying bow.

Tallulah scratched her head feathers with one foot. 'I've flown all the skies above the island and, well, Eagle Valley is the most . . . *unsettling.*'

Jim pointed south out to sea before turning to the animals. 'Look at those grey clouds. This sunshine is the calm before that storm. And it'll start getting dark in a few hours. We have no choice but to go through this valley. The thief came this way and went into the Craggy Caves, so we *must* get there to turn our lighthouse lights back on. We *have* to get there to save our island. Everything that lives here is *counting on us!*'

Even if, Jim thought, part of him *did* want the pirate ship to land here.

The group of animals looked at him.

'Rousing speech,' Rafi said. 'Though I still need some cheese.'

'LET'S GO!' Jim darted down the grassy incline, hundreds of flowers whipping past his legs as he ran into Eagle Valley. He bolted across the valley floor, Maximus clinging to his shoulder, Tallulah flying overhead, and Rafi and the Rigging Rats sprinting ahead of him.

A low, hollow screech rang out from somewhere inside the two rock-beak formations.

Rafi lifted his black-circled eyes to the sky, panic filling them. *'Must . . . run . . . faster!'* His little raccoon legs blurred as he bounded onward.

Another nail-scraping screech echoed across the valley.

Running hard, Jim saw six, seven . . . *eight* huge birds rise out of cracks in the giant rock-beaks, the birds' wingspans easily as wide as he was tall. Lowering his head, he tore towards the narrow, U-shaped dip of the valley that lay below the rock formations.

The Rock Eagles swooped down towards the group, and Jim gasped, now counting twenty huge birds of prey flying their way from the valley's opposite end.

'Maybe . . . they won't . . . attack us . . . if I give them . . . cheese?' Rafi puffed.

Jim snorted. 'And maybe we could ask them,' he darted left to avoid a rock, 'if they've seen a horned beast thief come this way?'

Running beneath the stone beaks stretching high above, the rocks' curved shadows turned the valley floor dark. A shiver shot down Jim's spine.

Tallulah swept across the valley, *ka-cawing* frantically as she swung left towards the base of one of the beak mountains, more Rock Eagles hot on her tail. She shot inside a thin crevice, the eagles too big to follow.

'Oh my . . . oh my . . . *we're all gonna DIIIIEEEEE!*' Rafi yelled, pelting his legs onwards into the valley's U-shaped floor.

'No, we are n—'

Jim's head whipped forward as a giant Rock Eagle *whooshed* over him. Ducking as he ran, the yellow-grey-black flash of talons missed his scalp by inches. *'Keep going, everyone!'* While he was running, he pulled the rusted cutlass from its scabbard.

A line of four Rock Eagles, soaring side by side, broke away from the larger group of twenty birds and swooped down up ahead, their screeches piercing Jim's ears. From the opposite end of the valley, they flew so low over the grass their talons sliced off flower-heads and, spreading slowly out across the width of the valley floor, the birds opened and snapped shut their beaks, aiming their flight paths directly towards Jim and the animals.

Jim skidded to a stop; his cutlass raised.

Rafi, Rum, Flum, Sum and Maximus slid to a stop beside him, panting and fixing their eyes on the incoming eagles.

Jim turned sideways-on, scrunching his feet into the ground. 'Get . . . *ready.*'

Rafi and the rats swivelled sideways-on too, whilst Maximus swirled all the feet on his left side.

The Rock Eagles flew at them at breakneck speed, like winged cannonballs.

'Hold your positions!' Jim curled his arms into the air, pointing the cutlass blade at the Rock Eagle flying straight at him.

'Oh no, oh no, oh no . . . I'm never going to eat anything ever again!' Rafi slapped his paws over his eyes.

Jim glared at the oncoming birds a hundred feet away, tearing four grass lines out of the valley floor. Fifty feet. Thirty feet. Ten feet.

Suddenly Tallulah swooped across the valley, parallel with the line of eagles, carrying something in her beak. Zipping over the top of the first bird, she let go. A sharp stone smacked the eagle downwards, and it crumpled into a ball of flapping wings.

Whooshing along above the second eagle, the little parrot dive-bombed, snapping her beak into the bird of prey's head. The eagle twirled upside down, barrelling in a sharp, blurry arc into the next eagle in line. Loud squawk-screeches echoed through the rock-beak formations as a tangle of wings, feathers and talons thudded into the ground.

Tallulah didn't stop. As the final eagle flew at Jim, Tallulah *ka-cawed* her defiance and drop-spun the tree branch she had in her claws; it sliced like a whirring blade into the eagle's face.

'*Aaaarkkk!*' the Rock Eagle screamed, reaching Jim just as Rum and Sum threw Flum into the air, his rat legs pin-wheeling, to punch the eagle in the eye. Hard.

The bird careered into a clump of mud, a plume of feathers and dirt spraying up . . .

. . . as Jim caught Flum in one hand, gently placing him back on the ground with his brothers.

Panting madly, Tallulah circled over them. 'K-keep running!' she called, flapping back up into the air.

High above the rock-beaks, Jim watched more eagles group together for a fresh attack. He, Maximus, Rafi and the rats fled through the valley as furious, hollow screeches reverberated down from above.

'*Run like the wind!*' Jim yelled, as they emerged out the other side of the rock-beaks' shadows. Racing up the valley's opposite hill, they glanced back, a wall of Rock Eagles soaring towards them, blotting out the storm-grey sky.

Sweat dripping down his forehead and with legs like jelly, Jim dropped to his knees in the grass. He heard Rafi yelling at him to keep running, and Maximus shouting in his ear, but an overwhelming cold rose like a heavy, dark thing inside him. Laying his cutlass on the ground, heart thudding in his mouth, all he could see were wings, talons and beaks shooting this way, and – frozen to the spot – he *knew* there was no way to escape the next eagle attack.

CHAPTER TWELVE

Jim knelt on the grass verge of Eagle Valley, sweat trickling down his face. The winged predators swooping towards him were the dark part of the island. And to fight dark, you had to think dark.

'*Huddle together!*' he screamed, snatching up his cutlass and beckoning the animals towards him. 'Let's make ourselves look bigger!'

Rafi leapt up into Jim's arms, nearly over-balancing him. Rum, Sum and Flum scampered up his leg – Rum squeezing in behind Jim's belt, Sum hanging onto his cutlass scabbard and Flum on his shoulder, hugging his neck next to Maximus. Jim stumbled as he felt small claws clutch the hair on his head and Tallulah's multi-coloured tail feathers hung over his face.

Together, Jim and his friends turned to face the

93

incoming Rock Eagles. His throat went dry as the long line of pointed beaks, open talons and spread-out wings swept over the valley grass towards them.

'No w-way can we take on that many!' Tallulah cawed, her voice breaking into a screech.

The grass flattened all around them.

Jim frowned, squinting through Rafi's fur to see a river of brown-black spilling out of the two rock-beaks. Coating the grasslands, a flood of swirling, tumbling ants was colliding in the valley's middle and surging all around them.

Rafi shivered in Jim's arms. 'Oh, good . . . we're going to be eaten by ants *as well!*'

'We are *not* bein' eaten by *anything*!' Maximus wriggled on to Jim's shoulder. 'I think . . . we're bein' rescued!'

The ant horde piled up into a wave of churning insect bodies, circling Jim and the animals. Closing in around Jim's feet, they tickled his skin as they swarmed up his legs. The ants surged through Rafi's grey-black fur, covered the Rigging Rats and marched up Jim's neck, pouring all over Tallulah, turning her bright colours into a writhing brown.

Then the rain started to fall.

A sheet of grey water hammered down on Jim and the animals, the attacking eagles becoming a blurry, black-white line just seconds away from them now.

Meanwhile, on seeing Maximus, the ants stopped. Every . . . single . . . ant halted.

'What's happening?' Jim mumbled through clenched, ant-covered lips.

'RISE!' Maximus yelled, his tiny voice carrying through the thundering rain.

In front of Jim, still carrying the animals, a writhing, jostling mound of ants grew out of the ground. Clambering on top of one another, the ants squirmed up into a blob shape, which quickly became a twenty-foot high, human-shaped ant-mass giant.

'Where are the eagles?' Rafi scratched at his ant-filled ears.

The ant-mass in front of them was so dense, Jim couldn't see the Rock Eagles either. And now the ant-mass was growing two arms shaped like massive hammers and—

Two eagles speared into the twisting ant-mass, both

bouncing off into the grass in flailing, feathery heaps. A third eagle sliced through the ants and out the other side, flying past Jim and his animal baggage. They watched as, laden with thousands of ants, the eagle's wings slowly stopped flapping, and it dropped to the ground with a *thud*.

'Whoa!' Rafi said, as the ants covering Jim and the others retreated to the ground to re-join the horde.

The next six eagles dive-bombed the huge ant-mass. Swinging its hammers right, left, up, down, the mass knocked all six birds out of the sky. More ants swarmed over the dazed eagles, hauling them away, back into the rock-beaks.

'*Yes!*' Maximus punched the air with thirty legs.

But one last Rock Eagle – bigger than the others – swooped in and around the ant-mass, ducking below its swinging hammers, its yellow beak wide open. It shot towards the ant-mass 'head' and, swallowing a wodge of ants, pummelled through and flew onwards, banking right towards Jim.

Click-clack.

The bird's talons tapped coldly together, its hollow screech piercing Jim's ears. The eagle barrelled through the air, snapping its beak at Tallulah who was still clinging to Jim's head as it shot over him. At the same time, the three Rigging Rats leapt off Jim's shoulders, and – with its eyes wide at seeing new prey – the eagle lunged at Flum and Rum and snapped its beak at Sum.

Jim yanked the Oskar-made steel hammer from his tool belt and whacked the eagle on the head, the bird dropping out of the air with a groan. It landed at Jim's feet as the ant-mass collapsed into a sea of bustling insects that swept underneath Jim and the animals. Still carrying Rafi, Maximus and Tallulah, Jim stumbled but stayed upright as the ants lifted them into the air. Surfing on the ants, up and out of the valley, towards the Craggy Caves, the Jim-animal huddle sped over the grass as it died away to become soil then weather-worn rocks.

'It's like we're flying!' Jim yelled, his arms numb from holding Rafi.

But soon the rocks under them turned into broken boulders before, up ahead, falling away to nothing.

Blue-white sea-spray burst into the sky.

Mixing with the rain, and the storm's rising wind,

the spray showered Jim and the animals with cold salty water as the ants kept pushing them forward.

'We're at the island's edge,' Rafi hollered, spitting seawater out of his mouth.

'The Barnacle Blowhole!' Maximus yelled, the loud *sssssshhhhhh* of spray drowning him out.

'We need the ants to stop!' Tallulah squawked. 'If they don't, we'll fall into the blowhole!'

Jim looked over at the sunken, half-moon hole carved into the cliff and *covered* in thousands of sharp-shelled barnacles.

The ant-mass turned towards it.

Rafi waved his short arms around. 'No, no, *NO!* How do we stop this ant ride?'

The ants sped up.

And, as they got closer to the hole, Jim's cheeks wobbling from the speed, the ant-horde swerved to form an arrow shape. An arrow pointing *to* the blowhole.

'Maximus!' Jim's heart thumped in his ears. 'Tell them to . . . to . . . *stop*!'

But it was too late. The ants threw Jim, and the animals clinging to him, into the gaping, black barnacle-toothed mouth of the blowhole.

CHAPTER THIRTEEN

A fresh jet of seawater sprayed into the air, soaking them as they soared down into the void. Separating from one another, Rafi screamed, Jim howled and Tallulah flapped up off his head, squawking. Rum, Flum and Sum clung together, dropping like a rat-comet.

Flying past the needle-like barnacles – missing them by inches – they fell into the blowhole's black heart, freezing air sweeping up Jim's legs, chest and face, sucking his breath away. He tumbled down through the damp darkness, finally hitting a slimy cushion of seaweed with a squelchy bounce.

'Aaaaarggghhhh!'

He whooshed down a slanted, seaweed-coated rock slide that funnelled him left, right and sharply straight again, spitting him out into a huge, underground black lake. Hitting the water fast, Jim skimmed across it, the animals following, spraying up white-water into one another's faces.

Eventually, they slowed to a stop, all treading water to stay afloat.

Jim licked his lips. Salty.

This lake was where the sea came in through the Craggy Caves entrance, hit the rock tunnel and jetted up out of the blowhole. Bobbing up and down, Jim glanced up at the domed, rugged ceiling stretching high above. Wispy, white flecks of light danced around on the rocks above, reflecting off the dark cave water.

He turned to break into a swim and his head smacked into something solid, lines jumping across his vision.

Rubbing his head dizzily, he looked up to see the lines were the wooden slats of . . . a boat.

'Edward's *jolle*!' Jim cried, blinking seawater out of his eyes and beckoning the floating animals over. Jim ran his hand along the roughly carved wooden hull.

'Are you getting in?' Tallulah cawed, flying over to sit on the boat's oar ring, preening herself.

Jim hauled himself up and over the side of the boat, collapsing in a sopping wet heap in the bottom. Two oars lay either side of him, and he picked them up as Maximus shakily crawled out of Jim's ear. The three rats leapt onto the boat's back seat, shaking their fur dry, and Rafi scrambled his soggy lump of a body over the boat's side, slapping down on the wood like a raccoon mop.

'Huh,' he huffed, 'nothing jolly about this boat here in a dark, dank, freezing cave!'

Jim rolled his eyes. 'Not *jolly*, Rafi, the boat's a *jolle*. Oskar told me it's what Edward called it when they carved it together, a long time ago.'

'Yes, *jolle* means a small craft cut out of one or two tree trunks,' Tallulah squawked.

'Well, what's it doing *here*?'

'It's usually moored at the Rigging Rats' beach,' Jim frowned. 'Maybe the filament thief stole this too? To get here?'

Rum, Flum and Sum clapped their claws, nodding frantically.

Grabbing a clump of his stomach fur, Rafi wrung out a stream of seawater. 'Are you telling me we've just traipsed across the whole island, almost got eaten by eagles, not had *anything* to eat so far, and yet the whole time the thief went *around* us to hide?'

Tallulah flicked a wing at the raccoon's ear. 'It was an *idea*, Rafi. Anything could have brought this boat here. Maybe the coming storm winds broke it loose from the beach and it just floated here.'

Rum, Flum and Sum clapped again, nodding more frantically.

Jim smiled at the rats, whilst Rafi lurched forward to tweak Tallulah's tail feathers. She squawked and skidded off her perch into the bottom of the boat. Wriggling around Jim's feet, her feathers tickling his toes, she flicked up a crinkled, water-marked parchment stuck to the boat's oar. Jim snatched it out of the air, pulling the paper up to his face. It was another of the posters, like the ones that had washed-up on Seal Cove. Except, unlike the wet one he'd kept in his breeches, *this one* wasn't smudged and he could read it all . . .

WANTED

Safe return of this Baby Boy.
To Ocracoke, North Carolina.

T'were lost
at sea near
Nassau,
the Year
of Our
Lord 1704.

REWARD

A King's Ransom of Treasure

If My Boy is harmed,
You'll be fed to the sharks!

Blackbeard

Jim stared at the sketch under the word 'WANTED' – a baby snuggled up inside a woollen hammock, hanging inside a barrel with the word 'Rum' branded on its side.

Looking like the half-drowned rat he was, Rum clambered on to Jim's shoulder and leant over the parchment, tapping the barrel with his forepaw before pointing at himself.

Jim smiled. 'No, Rum, I'm sorry. It's not yours. I think this barrel . . . was mine.'

Rum folded his front legs over his little chest.

Jim's throat went dry. 'So, does that mean my . . . my . . .' the parchment shook in his hands, '. . . my *father* is a pirate called—?'

Rafi snatched the paper out of Jim's hands, crumpled it up into a ball and threw it into the sea. 'We *don't* have time for reading!' he snapped, his little black eyes glinting. 'It's getting dark outside, the storm is coming, we *must* find the filaments . . . and I am VERY hungry! Possibly verging on *hangry*.'

Jim opened his mouth to protest, but he knew Rafi was right. He grabbed up the boat's oars. 'Come on. The thief *has* to be in these caves somewhere,' he said,

his voice echoing off the domed, stone roof as he tried not to think about what the parchment meant.

A faint chink of light twinkled to his left.

'Over there!' Jim speared the black water with the oars, rowing hard, the little boat jolting through the cave and sailing into one of the many dark tunnels.

The boat bobbed and wobbled through a long section of total pitch black. Jim couldn't even see Maximus on his shoulder, let alone the other end of the boat. But, gradually, the craggy cave roof began shimmering with lights. At first, Jim thought it was the seawater reflecting up onto the roof again, but as the cave got lower, he saw every light was moving.

'Pretty!' Rafi reached up with one paw, trying to touch the wriggling lights.

'*Awww-aaaahhh*,' Rum, Flum and Sum cooed together.

Tallulah rolled her eyes. 'Have you lot never seen glow-worms before?' She flapped upwards, gliding just below the worms clinging to the roof, their white-blue haze reflecting on her wing feathers.

'My fourth cousin's, twice-removed, sister's husband's son – Barry – is a glow-worm,' Maximus informed everyone.

'Guys, can we *please* focus on our mission?' Jim's voice was a watery echo.

The boat drifted under a huge, downward bulge in the cave's roof, forcing Jim to limbo his upper body backwards whilst keeping hold of the oars. All the animals ducked too, and with less than six inches of space above the boat's hull, Jim's nose rubbed against craggy rock, and several indignant glow-worms, before the roof opened back up.

Jim's jaw dropped as a new, waterlogged cave expanded out towards two gigantic, hourglass-shaped pillars of partly-submerged rock. The pillars were an entrance, dark water flowing between them, that led to a wider cave beyond.

The boat bobbed through the stalactite-stalagmite pillars, down a tiny waterfall and into a round cave. On its far side was a long, jagged ledge that rose up out of the rippling water, and dotted along the ledge were rows of needle-point stalactites jutting down from the roof. Thick stalagmites stretched up to meet them from the ledge floor, like a line of tiger's teeth.

The light Jim had seen earlier twinkled again on the ledge.

Jim pointed at it, then *shushed* them all with one finger to his lips. He rowed the boat to the nearest slab of low rock, the hull thudding against a stalagmite. He pulled himself and Maximus up onto the ledge, the rats, raccoon and parrot following.

Rustling filled the cave.

The sound made Jim's neck hairs stand up. 'What's . . . *that*?' he whispered, glancing around, but seeing nothing.

'It's the sound the deadly horned beast thief makes before it strikes down its prey!' Rafi hissed.

The three rats gulped.

'It's just sound behaving differently in the cave,' Tallulah chirped quietly, landing on the stumpy top of a damp stalagmite.

Jim picked Tallulah up, plonked her on his shoulder next to Maximus and crept along the ledge, past a row of stalactites and around the curved, back edge of the cave.

Ssssssssht-sssssssht.

He stopped, and pointed at the ledge's far end. A glowing, white light ebbed and flowed from behind a circle of stalactites and stalagmites.

'There!' he said, tiptoeing towards the eerie glow shining out between cracks in the stalactites.

'Is that . . . our . . . tungsten?' Maximus leant forward on Jim's shoulder.

Jim took a deep breath and, moving slowly towards the light, he whispered, 'Careful, if this is the thief, we know it's big, dangerous and devious . . . and it has horns!'

The glow radiating from the spiked, calcium jaws

of the stalactite-stalagmite circle was brighter now, pulsing like a slow heartbeat. And, as the animals and Jim snuck closer, a shadow flickered through a diamond-shaped gap in the circle. A shadow that got bigger and bigger, climbing up the cave wall. Jim swallowed.

It was the shadow of two huge horns.

'It's . . . it's . . . *massive*,' Rafi gulped, the shadow creeping up across the entire cave roof, dwarfing them all.

Jim wrapped his sweaty hand around his rusted cutlass hilt. Tightly. Pulling in a breath, and signalling to the others to get ready, he ducked through a gap between the stalactite-stalagmites and into the glowing, white light . . .

Chapter Fourteen

Jim stared down at an iridescent black-horned beetle, about the same size as Tallulah. It was sitting very still, two shiny black horns curling up and out from either side of its head, the light pulsating behind the beetle as it stared up at him.

'*You're* the giant horned beast?'

Rafi and the rats sidled up next to Jim and as Tallulah joined them, a long silence spread over them all as they looked at the beetle.

'Well, *that's* a let-down,' Rafi said, shaking his head.

The beetle swivelled, hissing at the raccoon. *Sssssssht-sssssssht.*

'Whoa, all right!' Rafi stepped back, holding up his paws. 'I didn't mean to hurt your feelings. I was just, well, expecting something a little . . . *scarier.*'

111

The beetle snapped its horns together, running at Rafi.

The raccoon climbed up the nearest stalagmite, trembling with panic. 'OK, OK, I'm sorry . . . you *are* scary. I see this now. But we come in peace!' Rafi glanced at the others, then at Jim. 'We do come in peace, don't we?'

Sssssssht-sssssssht.

The beetle scuttled back to its previous position, standing next to three, tiny strips of metal which glowed brightly. Jim sighed with relief, only looking at the pulsating tungsten for a moment it was so blinding.

Rafi turned to Maximus accusingly. 'You said the horned thief was huge.'

Maximus shrugged. 'To me, that beetle *is* huge!'

The giant beetle wrapped its two back legs and pygidium tail lump around the ends of the three stolen tungsten pieces and the metal strips glowed brighter. The metal's opposite ends were twisted around three tiny twinkling blue stalagmites no taller than Jim's thumb. Spread out from the beetle's legs, like three fork prongs, the glowing strips were stretched over a hole in the rock.

Jim dropped to his knees and slid forward, whispering gently to the black-horned beetle. 'It's all right, I'm not going to hurt you.'

The beetle hissed at him.

Inside the hole he saw twenty or thirty miniature black-horned beetles. Crammed in tightly together, hugging each other, all the baby beetles had their mother's iridescent sheen, sparkling green, blue and yellow from the metal's glow.

'So, this . . . *this* is why you're a thief.' Jim looked at the animals, and whispered, 'She's just keeping her babies warm.'

'*Babiiiiieeeeessss!*' Rafi rushed over and knelt beside Jim. 'Can I pick one up and stroke it?'

Jim glanced at him, rolling his eyes. 'How much do you think the mother beetle would like you to do that?'

The mother hissed at Rafi.

Rafi withdrew and Jim put a hand on the raccoon's shoulder. 'They are beautiful. But let's be gentle.'

'But, *but* . . . babiiieees,' Rafi looked at Jim. 'OK, yes, *gentle.*'

Jim watched several beetle babies wriggle around one another, snuggling up. It looked like the mother

113

beetle was using her own energy, combined with the sparkly rocks, to conduct heat that lit up the metal; the tungsten was keeping her babies warm in this remote, freezing, wet cave.

'The lighthouse bulb filaments are keeping them alive.' Jim looked at the other animals, all of them staring back, bemused.

Rafi's eyes brimmed with tears.

'Rafi? You all right?'

The raccoon sniffed, then blinked and blinked. 'Oh, it's just,' he slapped his paw over his heart, 'they make me . . . oh, just *look* . . . just look-ee-wook-ee-woo-woo at their clever-wever mummy keeping them all safe and warm-ee-woos and—'

Tallulah slapped Rafi across the ear with her wing. 'Get a grip! *That* beetle stole our metal, and we need it.'

Jim sighed. He knew Tallulah was right. They had to get the tungsten back to the lighthouse before the storm came and night fell. Touching the soggy parchment from Seal Cove in his breeches, he *also* knew that the pirate ship had to be turned away from Black Eel Rock and the island, despite the longed-for clues it had given him about his father in the world beyond. Yet,

how could they get the tungsten back when the beetle mother didn't know she had done anything wrong? She only wanted to keep her babies warm.

Jim lowered himself to the same height as the black-horned beetle mother, seeing the strong arch of her large, armoured back and the smooth, yet serrated curve of her frontal lobe horns. She lifted her legs up, flicking open the cases that covered her wings.

Ssssssht-sssssssht.

She didn't like him getting close, but he gritted his

115

teeth and stayed put.

'Listen,' he whispered, lying chest-down on the cold, damp cave ledge. 'I know your babies need to be safe . . . but we really must have that metal to keep hundreds of ships and our island safe too.'

The beetle mother flicked her wing-cases fully open with a loud *click-click-click*. Doing this made her look six times bigger, the shadow of a horned monster crawling up the cave wall.

'OK, *now* I see the huge, scary horned thief,' Rafi gulped, wide-eyed, and the three rats leapt back from the beetle mother, chittering.

Sweat prickled on Jim's forehead. 'We don't want to cause you any problems but . . .'

He felt something wiggling about in his hair and, a moment later, he went cross-eyed as his eyes followed Maximus's legs marching down his forehead, the ridge of his nose, lips, and chin, before leaping off his face and pitter-pattering across the rock.

Maximus stopped in front of the black-horned beetle mother, raising himself up. He cleared his throat. 'Believe me, I know how hard tis bringin' up children. I understand you want to hide them away until they're big enough to face the world. You're a carin' mother. But this bleak cave is no place for 'em to grow up. They need a *proper* home. One where they – and you – are *appreciated*.' Maximus glanced back at Jim and the other animals. They all nodded. 'Well, us lot . . . and some others . . . we *have* that home. Why don't you come live with us?'

The mother beetle *click-clacked* her horns together, glanced at her babies then back at the millipede, the iridescent sheen on her wing cases changing colour, the metal strips glowing brighter.

'Our home, the lighthouse, has a basement full of hard-workin' bugs,' Maximus continued. 'There are *so* many other beetles like you and your babies there, you'd never be alone. And we'd all help look after your children.'

Jim held his breath.

Silence in the cave.

Even the faint lapping of seawater against the rocky ledge quietened.

'Come on, Mama Beetle, what do you say?'

The beetle mother looked round at Jim, Rafi, Tallulah, Rum, Flum and Sum, pacing side to side but not far enough to break her link with the metal strips. She lifted and bowed her head a few times, then the three strips of tungsten faded from blinding white, to yellow, orange . . . and to a dull grey.

The beetle babies in the hole shuffled around, chattering to one another.

The mother shook her back-end and legs free of the metal strips, crouched down and sounded three gentle *clack-clack-clacks* into the hole. Immediately, all the baby beetles scuttled up the rock and onto their mother's back, all thirty tiny babies gripping under their mother's wing cases. She snapped her wings closed over them, and strode forward, head up and horns held high in the air.

Standing in front of Maximus, dwarfing him, the mama beetle leant down and, tenderly, rubbed the side of her head against Maximus's tiny millipede cheek.

Maximus returned the gesture, cooing.

Jim beamed, turned to the others – who were all smiling too – and slid across the rock to un-twine the strips of lightbulb metal from the stalagmites.

The mother beetle and her precious beetle baby cargo crawled over to Rafi and sat down in front of the raccoon.

Rafi held up his paws. 'Wh-why are you looking at me?'

The beetle mother flicked her wing cases apart, showing her babies.

Rafi frowned. 'What . . . do you want me to take you?'

The beetle mother nodded, her horns touching the rock.

Rafi laughed, clapping his paws and jumping up and down. He lowered himself to the ground and pushed his snout towards the beetle. 'Climb aboard, Mama!'

She scurried up Rafi's black-white face, snuggling down into the fur on his head.

'Oooh, she's so *warm*.'

Tallulah winced. 'Let's hope she and her babies make it back alive in that seven-year unwashed fur.'

Jim poked Tallulah, picked up Maximus and crawled back through the ring of stalactite-stalagmites, the Rigging Rats following.

'Let's get home and fix this!'

CHAPTER FIFTEEN

The tiny *jolle* boat, crammed full with Jim and the animals, burst from the mouth of the Craggy Caves and splashed into a swirling ocean. Jim gripped the oars as the churning, crashing waves snatched hold of them, the sky an angry black-grey overhead, with streaks of lightning skimming across the clouds.

Going around the island to get home faster had seemed like a good idea. But now, after rowing back the way they had come, then along another cave tunnel to get out here, the rain pouring down on them and the boat drifting close to the rocky cliffs, Jim wasn't so sure.

But they were running out of time.

Tallulah flew above the boat, her wings rocking from side to side in the wind; she squawked a warning to Jim when a big wave headed their way, but the ocean noise and thunderclaps drowned her out.

Jim's palms burned from the oar wood, but he kept rowing and the boat stayed on course. As the *jolle* sliced through another giant wave, a line of tall trees appeared on the clifftop – the edge of the Flaming Forest. Its flamingo colony would be sheltering from the storm in there somewhere.

They rowed slowly around the island's jagged circumference, trees giving way to swamps, then lower marshland, before lightning flickered over the beach with the tall, wrecked rigging mast embedded in its sand, where the rats lived and Oskar held his all-island meetings. They were heading the right way, towards Seal Cove, as a white-flared dance of dark lines, shapes and shadows lit up the whole island. Thunder roared across the ocean as the boat splash-landed off a wave, slamming Jim's stomach up into his throat.

'Urgh, the horizon won't keep still.' Rafi's face was a pale green.

They rose up on another giant wave, and Jim finally saw a tall, familiar silhouette. 'The lighthouse!'

All the animals glanced up to see the dark, beamless

lighthouse peeking over the crown of the clifftop. A smile crept across Jim's seawater-lashed cheeks.

Wind howled across the boat, smacking it sideways.

Both oars were ripped out of Jim's hands and they speared into the churning sea, splintering. *'Noooo!'* he cried, scrambling around in the bottom of the boat, looking for something else to use.

The *jolle* shunted right, then left, skimming across the water.

Rafi clamped his paws over his eyes.

Jim grabbed the boat's stern, the wood shaking . . . *trembling* . . . under his hands.

FNOOOOOOOOAAAAAAAAAAARRRRRRRRRR!

A foghorn echoed across the island, and rolled over the sea.

'Elsa!' Jim scanned the clifftop, looking for the elephant as a tangle of brown seaweed slapped him across the face. A second seaweed tentacle flew out of the ocean, wrapping itself around Rafi's neck, then three, four, five, six seaweed clusters wet-slapped on to the boat, snatching up Rum, Flum and Sum, and whipping Tallulah out of the air, on to the boat.

A slimy seaweed limb curled around Jim's leg and,

as he tried to tug it free, the tentacle clamped around his skin even tighter.

'Watch out, it's Snagging Seaweed!' he yelled as the seaweed began dragging him and the animals towards the side of the boat and the raging sea.

'Do something, Jim!' Maximus roared, sheltering in Jim's earlobe.

Jim tried to grab the hilt of his cutlass but more seaweed slid around his wrist, yanking his hand off the cutlass hilt, the rusted sword sliding back inside its scabbard.

'No!'

Jim sank his teeth into the seaweed, whilst Tallulah did the same, nibbling a strand with her beak, flapping erratically around the boat. The Rigging Rats were busy gnawing at the brown limbs clinging to them.

With the lighthouse so close, it meant Seal Cove beach was just minutes away, and if Jim could only get . . . his . . . cutlass . . .

Meeeeewwwww! A screech exploded across the boat as a skinny, furry, sea-drenched cat skidded into the stern. *Mew-mew-eeeeeeee!*

'Claudette!' shouted Jim. 'How . . . what . . . oh I'm so glad to see you!'

Claudette's fur stuck out in soaked spikes as she jumped onto Jim's lap, snarled and clamped her jaws around the hilt of his cutlass. Digging her claws into Jim's legs, the black cat crawled backwards, pulling the heavy cutlass out of its scabbard.

Ssshhiiiiiiing.

'Go, cat!' Rafi croaked through a neck-wrap of seaweed.

Clank!

The cutlass' blade hit the boat's hull and, with his free hand, Jim grabbed the hilt and swung it down on the seaweed tentacles around his leg and wrist, cutting the seaweed and snapping the tendrils back into the sea.

'Yaaaaaar!' He held his cutlass in the air, the storm battering against him as he dived at Rafi and slid the cutlass blade up under the raccoon's neck fur, slicing the seaweed off. He nicked Tallulah's feet free of her slimy trap, before swinging round to carefully cut through the seaweed tentacles wrapped around Rum, Flum and Sum.

Shivering with relief, all the animals stared at Claudette gratefully as white-veined lightning criss-crossed the night sky, making her green eyes glow.

'Thank you, Claudette,' Jim breathed, 'we'd have been done for without you.'

Above them, thunder roared, and wind surged over the boat, slamming it across the water as if it were a pebble thrown by a giant. Jim and the animals tumbled into one another, the *jolle* bouncing off one wave and ploughing into another, the lighthouse flying into view, then slipping away again.

Seal Cove was near now. The boat just needed to hold together for—

Jim looked over and saw the biggest wave he'd ever seen coming towards them. 'HOLD ON, EVERYONE!' he shouted.

Rusted nails burst out of the boat's wooden slats, water jetting up into the hull. Jim's stomach jolted into his throat as the gigantic wave lifted the *jolle* up into the air. The boat flew through the dark, clouded sky into a sudden, eerie silence.

Jim and the animals screamed.

The twisting grey ocean disappeared and all they could see was the cliff-side. Hurtling at the rocks, Jim gripped his cutlass and Claudette, his heart thudding hard, but suddenly the boat lurched vertically upright, pinning them all to its floor, a blur of jagged rocks and slate-coloured sky shooting by. Jim caught sight of a long, unfurling grey trunk as the boat cruised over the clifftop, and a moment later, the *jolle* thudded down onto rain-soaked grass. Everyone rattled around as the hull slid forwards, Elsa galloping beside them, lifting her trunk up to blast a deep, echoing trumpet-roar that rumbled across the island.

Tallulah flapped herself free of the boat, as it careened across the clifftop field, towards the lighthouse.

'Time to jump ship!' Rafi hollered, gripping the beetle-mother on his head tightly.

The boat's stern carved a trench across the lighthouse lawn, mud and grass spraying into their faces, the front door shooting towards them.

'Brace for impact!'

CRACK!

The *jolle* hull split down the middle, its two wooden sides collapsing open like a chopped apple, with Jim and the animals thudding into one another – legs, arms, fur, hands, paws, claws and feathers tumbling in a heap next to the lighthouse.

Elsa leant over them, her warm eyes looking down at the pile of out-of-breath animals and boy. 'Nice cup of tea, everyone?'

CHAPTER SIXTEEN

But there was no time for tea. Not yet, at least.

Jim crawled to his feet and glanced across at the tumbling, smashing chaos of the sea. The storm had taken hold, and full darkness was less than an hour away. Jim turned to smile at Claudette and Elsa. 'Thank you, both! You saved us,' Jim said, as Elsa ruffled his hair with her trunk and Claudette shook a shower of seawater over his ankles. 'But now . . . *we have to get the bulbs working!'*

Oskar swung out of the lighthouse door, scratching his head at the broken boat and pile of groaning animals, before turning his beady eyes to Jim and raising two questioning eyebrows.

Jim smiled, rummaging inside his tool belt to pull out the metal strips.

'Well done!' Oskar said, patting Jim's shoulder. 'Quickly, we must melt the tungsten back in place inside the bulbs.'

'How can we do that?'

'My soldering fire ants are ready to go, up in the Lantern Room. But they hate the rain, so I *hope* they will want to work.' The orangutan hurried inside the lighthouse, swinging up the spiral staircase. 'Come as fast as you can!'

Jim held open the lighthouse door, but before he could head inside with the others, the beetle mother scuttled across the wet grass towards him, stopped at his feet and glanced up as she clicked her huge black horns together.

Jim looked around for Maximus, but the millipede was no longer on his shoulder. As the beetle mother *clack-clacked* up at him, he saw the tail-end of about sixteen legs disappearing down a hole in the lighthouse's wall; an entrance to the bug basement.

'Must go see the wife, or my life won't be worth livin'!' the millipede yelled.

The beetle mother rammed her horns into Jim's ankle.

'Um . . . *ow*!' He lifted up his ankle, clutching it. 'That actually hurt!'

'I don't speak beetle, but she seems pretty upset with you,' Rafi said, shaking seawater all over Jim.

'Thanks Rafi, that's *really* helpful . . . and please, can *everyone* stop using me as a towel?' Jim leant over the beetle as she *rat-a-tat-tatted*, running at his other ankle. He jumped aside. 'I'm sorry,' he said to the beetle mother, 'but we *must* get the lighthouse beams out across the bay. Perhaps you and your babies could head down to the basement to—'

The beetle mother rammed her horns into his other ankle, then scuttled inside the lighthouse.

'Great. Good talking with you,' Jim winced.

Elsa marched around the lighthouse, stamped her foot on a metal lever in the grass and a circular, stone platform glided out of the base. She climbed on board as it rose up the lighthouse's side to where the wall opened outwards from her room, and she strolled inside.

Tallulah cawed, flying up to the Lantern Room's domed, glass roof and the rats chittered to one another, scurrying through Jim's legs and into the lighthouse after Rafi.

For a moment Jim stood at the door in the wind and rain. Something in the distance caught his eye, out past the cliff edge overlooking Seal Cove. The hairs on the back of his neck rose up and, through a rain-lashed night sky and swirling waves, Jim saw a murky silhouette out beyond Black Eel Rock. The pirate ship; it was heading for the rocks. 'Oh *NO!*'

He turned and followed his friends up the stairs, three at a time. Round and round he went, panting as he reached the Lantern Room. Bright white lightning forked across the grey-black sky. It lit up the ocean and the ship being jostled towards Black Eel Rock.

'Jim, are you with us?' Oskar snapped his fingers in front of Jim's face. 'The fire ants refuse to leave their nest . . . we *must* think of a different solution.'

Jim shook himself from the hypnotic chaos outside and looked at the spinning, wooden-wheeled lighting gantry.

'We may not have to.' He pointed up. 'Look!'

The orangutan turned and gasped.

Scurrying all over the gantry, where the three

huge lightbulbs jutted up from their metal housings, were the baby beetles. The lanterns looked alive with a rippling, iridescent beetle-skin flowing over their surfaces. And, in the midst of this frantic insect activity, stood the black-horned beetle mother next to the circular, metal coupling of one lightbulb. She bent down to grasp the bulb's delicate, rounded bayonet connector between her pincers, lifting it up and out of its holding.

Jim's throat went dry.

The bulb, easily six times bigger than the beetle, and made of thin glass, wobbled as she pulled it clear of the electrical holder.

All the animals stared up at the beetle, open-mouthed. Except for Claudette. She was sitting, licking her paw, next to Norman the mole's little pot, waiting below the on/off lever.

'The strips of tungsten!' Oskar said, rolling his long fingers out to Jim who was gawping up at the lighting gantry.

'She stole the filaments like this . . . but how did she—'

Oskar blew a raspberry in Jim's face. 'Focus, Jim. Give . . . me . . . the . . . filaments!'

'Oh yes, right,' and Jim unfolded his clenched fist, handing the three, hair-width strips of metal to the orangutan.

Oskar bounded over to the lighting gantry, handed one metal strip each to Rum, Flum and Sum, and stood back as the three Rigging Rats scampered up the gantry. Rum leapt nimbly to the bulb the mother beetle was clutching, its glass swaying precariously in the air above her. The little rat, avoiding stepping on the beetle babies scurrying around his feet, climbed up inside the bulb's electrical coupling. His whiskers twitching, Rum gently laid the thin strip of tungsten between the two points where the electricity would flow.

The Rigging Rat backed out, and Jim gasped as the beetle mother's two front incisors began to glow. In seconds they went from orange to white, radiating so much heat that Jim could feel it on his cheeks.

'So *that* is how she did it.' Oskar nodded to himself. 'When she stole the tungsten, she lifted the bulb glass up and used her . . . *energy* . . . to snap the metal off. She is amazing! And now, I hope, she will reverse this . . .'

Whilst she gripped the bulb's glass, holding it in the

air with her horns, the mother beetle edged inside the coupling.

Jim held his breath.

The beetle leant towards one end of the metal strip and, with a burst of white sparks she touched her glowing incisors against the metal. Then she scuttled across to melt the tungsten's other end, a whiff of burning metal filling the Lantern Room. She scampered out, lowered the glass bulb case over the holding, and went on to fix the other two bulbs in the same way.

'Whoa . . .' Jim let out a breath.

'Amazing!' Rafi shook his head.

'*Very* clever,' Oskar agreed, clapping with the pride of a fellow technician.

Tap-tap-tap-tap.

Jim looked round, seeing Tallulah's feathers blowing around outside the window as she clung to the wind swept balcony, tapping the glass with her beak. The parrot jabbed a wing out to sea, pointing into the darkness.

The ship.

'We have to get the beams on NOW!' Jim cried, catching Sum as the rat leapt from the gantry.

'We must get out of the Lantern Room before Norman flicks the switch.' Oskar swung towards the balcony door and Jim followed, a blast of freezing wind knocking him and the animals backwards.

Jim held onto the door as all his friends hurried out into the stormy night, the beetle babies scurrying back under their mother's wing cases as she ran.

Behind him, he saw Claudette had that mischievous twinkle in her green eyes. She turned away, yawned and stretched, before knocking on Norman the mole's pot and then idling back to Jim.

'Don't rush,' he smiled as she rubbed past his leg and together they stepped outside onto the shuddering, wet balcony.

None of them saw Norman do his lever pull-down duty, blissfully unaware there had ever been a problem with the lantern. Within a couple of seconds the three lighthouse bulbs burst into life. A solid, yellow beam swept out across the swirling sea to the horizon. Breaking through rain, and thick, cloudy darkness, the light hit Black Eel Rock and lit up its twisted, shadowy contours.

Jim and the animals jumped up and down on the balcony, cheering and clapping. The seals down in their cove grunted an *arf-arf-arf* chorus up at the storm. Claudette sat beside Jim as they watched the lighthouse beams sweep across the bay, lighting up the monstrous waves that crashed into Black Eel Rock, smacking the ship back and forth . . .

. . . before, a few tense moments later, it slowly turned its stern away, sailing back out to sea.

Jim glanced around at all the animals standing with him at the top of their lighthouse. Oskar nodded at him and curled a big, hairy arm around his shoulders. Hugging each other tight, the orangutan and the boy looked out at the vast, dark sea.

Somewhere, out past the horizon, the lighthouse beam finally ended on a patch of black, moon-flecked ocean. And there, projected onto a wave, lay a faint silhouette of a boy, an orangutan, a parrot, an elephant, three rats, a raccoon . . . and, if you looked closely enough, a tiny millipede who had climbed up to the balcony to be with his friends.

CHAPTER SEVENTEEN

As the wind howled outside, rattling the lighthouse windows, Elsa wiggled her bottom through the living room door. Carrying a tray of hot, crushed mango juices – with dollops of cream on top – she plonked herself down on the floor, next to the fireplace.

Orange sparks flew up the chimney as Rafi jabbed the fire with the poker.

With Claudette asleep on his lap, Jim reached across from the battered sofa for a steaming mug. Sipping it, he felt the mango heating his belly and the fire warming his skin. He closed his eyes for a moment, sighing, before smiling at the three Rigging Rats, all strewn across the rug, belly-up, snoring; their tiny mugs of mango juice lying empty beside them.

It was cramped inside the lighthouse's round little

living room, but it was cosy and felt *right* to be in here with all his friends after everything they'd been through.

Oskar sat in a ragged, sea-salt-stained leather chair that had once belonged to a Spanish galleon captain before his ship was smashed to pieces by Black Eel Rock. He slurped his hot mango crush. Pulling the mug away from his mouth, an orange-white cream moustache covered his top lip. He looked at Jim, smiling widely.

Jim snorted a laugh, burying his face in the cream on top of his mug. He brought his head back up, going cross-eyed at the bubbling mound of mango-mush sitting on his nose. He smiled at Oskar, the cream dribbling down his chin.

'A beard will suit you, when you are old enough to grow one,' Oskar nodded.

'Just not a white and orange one!' Tallulah cawed from her perch up on the curtain rail.

Oskar frowned, rubbing his chin hairs. 'There is nothing wrong with orange-white hair!'

'No, it is very dashing on you, dear.' Elsa noisily sucked a whole mug of hot mango up her trunk.

'I think a big, furry black beard would cap off Jim's look nicely,' Rafi smirked.

Oskar shot the raccoon a look.

Jim rubbed the mango-cream off his face. 'Guys, I don't want a beard! They look . . . *itchy*. Anyway, I'm *twelve*, beards are for old people.' Tallulah burst into a cawing, parrot-laugh, as Jim looked across at Oskar. 'You know, apart from Elsa's paintings of Edward, I've never seen another human from the world beyond.'

Oskar rested his mug of steaming mango on a chair arm. The orangutan glanced around the tiny living room, all eyes staring back at him. He shuffled his tool belt up his stomach and leant forward. 'Some of them are tender, kind souls. Like Edward. But many . . . are not.'

'That's the same for animals.' Jim glanced out of the living room window, the rain streaming across it. 'You're all wonderful. But . . . the Rock Eagles.'

Oskar shook his head. 'The eagles go with their instincts. They act bloodthirstily to feed themselves, to protect their babies. To stay safe. To *survive*. As do many animals. But humans, hmm . . .' Oskar pushed his round glasses up his nose. 'You see, Jim, some humans become desperate and do awful things. Others are worse than that. They *choose* to be bad.'

'And my parents . . . which were *they*?' Jim peeled his fingers off the mug's handle; he was gripping it so tightly his skin had turned white. 'I know I keep on about the story of how I arrived on the island, but I've often thought that . . . well . . . my father *must* have been bad to abandon me. To shove me into a barrel of rum and push me out to sea . . . yet the parchment says Blackbeard is looking for me. Who is Blackbeard?'

Oskar stared at him, pursing his lips.

Jim looked at Elsa. She looked down into her mug. Jim glanced at Rafi. The raccoon blinked several times, turning away to poke at the fire again. Tallulah said nothing. And when he looked down at his lap, he saw Claudette quickly close the eye she had just opened.

Rummaging in his breeches for the soggy poster, Jim said, 'I'm glad you taught me to read.' He flicked the paper free of his waistcoat, dripping water on Claudette's ears. 'But I still don't understand what all of this means. There's a drawing of me and it says I'm wanted "safely returned".' Jim held the parchment out towards Oskar. 'And look at the words underneath – where's Ocracoke and Nassau? Are these real places, where I'm from? This Blackbeard, are these words written by—'

Cracked shards of mug imploded inside Oskar's fist. Hot mango crush splattered all over the leather chair, rug and mantelpiece. The orangutan grunted, flicked the remains of the mug into the fire and stomped out of the room.

Jim swallowed, tears welling in his eyes.

Elsa was already clearing up the mess. 'I think we could all do with a nice sleep, dearies.'

Claudette ran silently from the room, the rats following, all rubbing their sleepy eyes. Tallulah soared out of the door, and Rafi opened his mouth to say something.

'That *wasn't* a question, dear,' Elsa snapped, and Rafi scampered from the room.

Elsa glanced over at Jim, holding the tray of mugs in her trunk. 'Don't worry, dear. He'll come round. He just cares for you more than anything. And asking those questions . . . well, for him, it's . . . difficult.'

Jim clenched his teeth to stop the tears falling. 'I . . . I'm sorry. I just wanted to know a little more. To see who I am and where I—'

'Get some rest, deary.' The elephant squeezed back out of the living room door. 'You'll feel a lot fresher in the morning!'

Wood crackled on the fire, spraying a line of sparks up the chimney. Jim glanced at it, sighing as he sat in the room on his own, looking down at the parchment in his hand. Maybe it was better he didn't know about where he came from; perhaps the human world wasn't *his* world. He went to throw the parchment in the fire.

'Don't you dare,' a small voice said from above.

Jim snapped his head up to the porthole windowsill. Maximus was sitting with forty-eight of his crossed legs dangling over the windowsill edge. Jim hadn't even known the millipede was in the room.

'Now see, young Jim . . . you're rightly entitled to know where yer from.' Maximus raised himself up and glanced out at the stormy night, before looking back at Jim. 'Unlike all of us, you weren't born on this 'ere island. Which makes you different. Special. And when you bring up as many kids as me, it teaches you things. Mostly, that – no matter what you say as their parent – children have to find their *own* way.

'And, young man, let me tell you . . . it were your *mother* what put you in that barrel of rum and sent you away. So, if that parchment holds clues to yer past . . . go solve 'em.'

Chapter Eighteen

Later that night, when the winds had calmed and the rain had stopped, Jim sat outside alone on the cliff edge. He looked out at the ocean, and up at the sweeping lighthouse beams.

One, two, three . . . three and a half.

Everything was back as it was supposed to be.

Except – he pulled the parchment up to his face – it didn't feel that way.

Looking down at the sketch of the baby and the word 'WANTED', it reminded him of all the times today the animals had tried to stop him reading the poster. First, the seals, when the parchments washed ashore; then Oskar out on the cliffs; Rafi in the Craggy Caves and, finally, Oskar storming off and Elsa telling him to go to bed rather than answer his questions about it.

Jim licked his dry lips, his hands shaking as he saw Oskar's mug imploding in his mind. He let out a long breath, looking at the dark sea. Seeing the orangutan so angry scared Jim – why wouldn't he talk about it?

Jim shivered. Standing in front of the endless ocean, he felt small. Like a nothing boy. A nothing boy, on a nowhere island. Was it *really* so important he know more about the world beyond?

He thought about the pirate ship sailing away and how it had taken answers about his parents with it. He wiped his sleeve over his brow as something glinted on the parchment. It was difficult to see out here under the night sky, even after he'd pulled it up to his face, but Jim saw *another* mark underneath the poster's 'WANTED' message. Turning the parchment sideways to try and read what the hidden note said, he glanced right.

A silhouette on the cliff edge slid into view.

He frowned, blinking. What was that?

The silhouette lit up as a lighthouse beam soared by overhead. Then it was gone again.

Jim froze.

Another beam swept by, illuminating half the silhouette.

Jim's heart sped up and he scrambled to his feet.

The silhouette stood on two legs.

He shook his head, looking away out to sea. He was seeing things and really should have gone to bed earlier, when Elsa had told him to.

Another beam flicked over the two-legged form, closer now. It must be one of the animals from another part of the island. Perhaps a huge flamingo was lost, or a lemur was walking on its back legs so it looked like . . .

The flash of one eye in half a silhouetted face.

Jim swallowed. This . . . *thing* had long, straggly hair and was walking slowly along the clifftop, beam after beam rhythmically lighting up half its stocky body and one of its legs.

This was . . . *impossible.*

'Hello, young man, it's all right, you're not dreaming,' the silhouette said, its voice echoing over the sound of the ocean. The face, the build, the voice. This was another . . . *human.* And, from what Oskar had told him of humans, this was a woman-female.

Jim opened his mouth to reply, but closed it again. Was this a ghost? Some kind of sea demon posing as a human to lure him into the water? He quietly placed a hand down to his cutlass hilt, gripping it tight.

'There's no need to be frightened, little one,' the human person said. Lifting up one hand, smoothly, she then lowered it again, slowly. Jim recognised this gesture – Oskar used it in a calming way to stop arguments. So, humans were like animals!

'Honestly, I am not going to hurt you.' The shadows across the human woman's face faded as she came closer to Jim. She had bright white skin, with no hairs on it as a human man like Edward did in his portraits, and her sharp blue eyes had a hard edge to them.

Jim smiled. Oskar's stories of humans *talking* like animals were true too.

'Why would I think you'd hurt me?' Jim breathed out through his nose, slowing his heartbeat. Just because this was his first contact with a human person from the world beyond, it didn't mean he had to be nervous. This was his island. He glanced around. Besides, she was on her own, whereas *he* had a whole lighthouse full of animals nearby to call if anything bad happened. 'How . . . how did you . . . where did you come from?'

'I'd like to ask you a question first, little one.' The woman slid a hand through her hair, squinting at him. 'What are you doing here on this island, all alone?'

Jim frowned. 'That's a strange question. I'm not alone! I have all the others here with me. There's Oskar, Rafi, Tallulah, Elsa, Maximus, Claudette and—'

'There are that many people here?' Her eyes widened.

Jim laughed. 'No, don't be silly. You're the first person I've ever met. They're animals. Oskar, Rafi, Tallulah and everyone . . . they're my family. We run the lighthouse together.'

Jim instantly knew Oskar would be annoyed at him for telling this woman so much. But she was his first person. And she was . . . nice. Also, he thought, she was a little stupid if she thought he ran the lighthouse all on his own!

The woman tilted her head to the side, raising one eyebrow. Jim hid a smile . . . the humans really did do the same things as animals.

'Ah,' she rubbed her chin, 'animals. Yes, of *course.*' There was a long silence, where she seemed to be thinking hard about what she wanted to say. 'I guess . . .

being here for twelve years on your own would make anyone imagine animals, plants, fish . . . maybe even the odd rock,' she cackled at this, 'were their friends!'

Jim stepped back. He didn't like how she laughed.

'Who *are* you?' He narrowed his eyes, glancing up at the lighthouse door. 'Where have you come from?'

'Well, young man, I'm someone who can help you escape your loneliness! And, besides, I've been looking for you . . . *for a very long time.*' She stepped closer to him, seizing his wrist in her hand.

Jim shrugged off her grip. 'Let go of me. I'm not going anywhere with you. I don't know *who* you are. This is my *home.*' He pointed to the lighthouse, the parchment flapping around in his hand, glistening in the moonlight.

The woman snatched it from his hands. 'What have you here? Oh, so you *do* know about us and that you are a wanted—'

'What?' Jim grabbed the parchment back and ran along the cliff edge, the words *'you do know about us'* ringing in his head. He quickly scanned the parchment again, squinting at it as he swung it up into the air.

A lighthouse beam lit up a streaky line in the

parchment's middle.

Breath caught in Jim's throat.

Raising the parchment above his head, in line with the beams, he saw *lots* of watermarks on the poster – lines, dots, words . . . all written *within* the paper, all leading to a big 'X' drawn inside a shape. A shape that looked like the outline of the island.

Was 'X' the location of a clue to his past? He strained his eyes at the paper. It *looked* like the 'X' was drawn where the lighthouse stood.

'So, it's a map . . .' Jim whispered, another beam lighting up the poster a bright yellow.

'Aye, tis that. Yer be catchin' on quick, lad!'

The map in Jim's hands was sliced in half by the curved blade of a cutlass as it was swung down to the grass. Jim leapt backwards, staring at a thin, ragged human man with long hair, both halves of the map curling up into the air and fluttering over the cliff. Trying to catch them, Jim pin-wheeled his arms in frantic circles, tipping backwards.

'Grab 'im . . . *quick!*' the man grasping the cutlass yelled.

Jim was yanked back onto the grass by the woman.

'Oh . . . *no* . . .' The woman's eyes widened as *she* lost her footing, toppling backwards over the cliff.

'Fer goodness' sake!' the man yelled, tutting, and flicked his arm at Jim. 'Don't just stand there, lad, grab 'er!'

Jim leapt to the edge, tugging her arm to pull her back upright. She grunted, brushed herself down, and nodded at him.

'Right, now we've all finished fallin' over the bleedin' cliff . . .' The man, standing above Jim had black rims around his eyes, and a grey beard tied into

two separate tails with twine.

Jim was shaking now; this man was terrifying, with sea-stained clothes, rotten teeth and a cutlass . . . 'Are you a-a—?'

'A shockingly good-looking man? Aye, tis true.' The man grinned, pulling his cutlass up out of the grass and slicing it twice through the air, before pressing the blade, hard, against the skin of Jim's neck.

Jim stepped back.

'You're Jim Rogers, ain't yer?' Two-beards bared his teeth.

Jim backed farther away, but bumped into the woman and she grabbed his arms.

'How do you know . . . where did you both . . . are you from the pirate ship that I saw leave?'

Two-beards thrust the cutlass tip at Jim's neck. 'Stop askin' questions!'

The woman knocked the blade from Jim's throat. 'Cap'n, you know he told us not to harm the boy.'

Two-beards glared at her, before turning back to Jim, lifting his cutlass up again in warning. 'Now, listen ter me—'

153

'I'm not going *anywhere* with you!' Jim blurted. 'How did you get on the island?'

'Feisty one, ain't yer!' Two-beards shoved Jim with such force he collapsed through the woman's arms onto the grass.

'Ow, that hurt!'

Two-beards' creaky laughter echoed over the cliffs. 'Oh diddums, and there's me a-thinkin' you were a big boy now. Bigger than ye were on the poster, at any rate.' Two-beards narrowed his eyes at Jim. 'Let us be startin' again, eh? I present, in your company this evenin', meself . . . Cap'n Charles "Two-Beards" Slayne. Behind ye is Annie Thache, me quartermaster. Short but mighty, she be.'

'*She* can also talk for herself,' Annie snapped.

Slayne opened and closed his mouth like a mute goldfish. 'Yes, well. Anyway! Tha rest o' me low-life, good fer nuthin' scumbag crew are on their way here, as I speak.'

Annie lifted Jim back up and he wriggled in her arms, his heart thudding.

Slayne snarled at him. 'We know who y'are, lad, and you're a-comin' with us.'

Jim threw his weight back against Annie, pushing her arm off him. He stepped forward and glared at the pirate captain, arms folded over his chest. 'I live here, on the island. And I don't want to leave.'

Slayne raised one pointy eyebrow to the night sky. 'Then why, pray tell, if yer love it here so much, are ye out at night all by yerself, a-lookin' at a secret map from the world beyond, eh?'

Jim blinked.

Slayne leaned his neck to the side, cracking his joints.

'Captain,' Annie intervened, 'I would counsel against revealing too much about how we got here and why we are here because—'

'That map,' Slayne said, ignoring his quartermaster, 'the one a-blowin' out ta sea on the wind, is over twelve years old.'

Annie shuffled from side to side, looking uncomfortable.

'It has a sketch of me arriving here. It talks of a reward, of treasure,' Jim said.

Slayne's cheek twitched. 'Aye. That's a-cause we have bin lookin' fer you,' the pirate wiped sweat off his brow, 'for twelve long bleedin' years, boy.'

Slayne's lips trembled, and the strain in his eyes was clear.

'But, why?'

Slayne cackled. 'Because, lad, *you* are the treasure.'

CHAPTER NINETEEN

'You're worth *a lot* of money,' Annie said, not meeting Jim's eyes. 'To us . . . and our ship's crew.'

He stared at her. Oskar had tried to explain about money and how it made the world beyond work. But Jim still didn't understand.

Slayne shoved his face right up to Jim's. 'Yer see, lad, A "King's Ransom" be a hefty sum, especially fer some poor, lowly, misfit pirates!'

'Misfits?' Annie huffed. 'Says the man who ties his beard in two.'

One of those beard-ties tickled Jim's chin, and he backed away from Slayne.

'This "King's Ransom" better be enough for us all, cap'n,' she said, as Jim felt her fingernails sink into his shoulder-blades.

'Annie, you know better than anyone how bleedin' much he wants this 'ere boy back.' Slayne turned to her. 'He'll pay up handsomely.'

Jim opened his mouth to speak, but Annie slammed a hand over it. 'Now we've found the boy, let's hurry up and get off this— *OW*!' She clutched the finger Jim had just bitten.

Jim shook free, running up to Slayne. 'Is it my father who wants me back?'

Slayne blinked at the shrillness in Jim's voice. 'Yes, yer father, o' course, lad.'

Jim stared at Slayne, his heart pounding and his skin tingling, one hand on his cutlass.

'Now, steady on, boy . . .'

Jim's breath hissed out through his teeth.

'Despite everythin', yer father ain't all bad,' Slayne said quietly, looking at the ground.

Annie spat a sharp laugh.

'Ee's a committed, smart man.' Slayne looked in every direction, but at Jim.

Annie snorted. 'Let's just get out of here, shall we?'

'Hell's blazes, woman! There ain't no rush. Not after twelve *bleedin' years*. There's no one else on this 'ere island, but the boy, us, the odd bird, monkey and a crab or two. We checked after we landed our ship, remember?'

Jim glanced up at the lighthouse, the smashed *jolle* remains still scattered on the front lawn. So, these pirates must have sailed their ship around the island's north side when the lighthouse lanterns were switched on again, and somehow landed somewhere else on the island. He wished he was up in his cosy bedroom with Rafi below him in his room and Elsa above him in hers. Thoughts tumbled through his mind.

He looked at Slayne's scrawny, dark-eyed, weather-battered face.

The animals had known someone like this man would come for him. How, Jim wasn't sure. But they had known.

He looked at Annie, his nostrils flaring. These people were pirates. And they had hunted him down . . . *for money*. He shivered. They were dangerous to him, the animals and the island.

Oskar had been right about humans; *this* was why he got upset when Jim asked about his parents.

Slayne narrowed his eyes at him. 'I a-see by yer

eyes that you're putting two 'an two together, lad. But whatever you're thinkin', put it out yer mind, because you're coming with us. Back to the real world. Back to where you belong. You're my ticket to retirement, boy, and ain't *nuthin'* stopping me from getting what I'm owed for you.'

'What *we're* owed.' Annie glared at Slayne.

Jim tasted sour bile in his throat, his belly clamping into a knot. He had to do something.

He kicked his foot, hard, into Annie's shin, then Slayne's too, and bolted across the lighthouse lawn. Cupping his hands over his mouth as he ran, he *screech-squawked* three times, the sound ripping across the island, echoing out over Seal Cove.

'Stop that bleedin' racket and get back here!' Slayne huffed, rubbing his shin before he and Annie sprinted after Jim.

Jim *screech-squawked* three more times.

Overhead, somewhere in the sky, Tallulah *screech-squawked* three times back.

Annie leapt at Jim, but he zig-zagged out of the quartermaster's clutches and she ploughed head-first into the pile of hay at the end of Elsa's elephant slide.

'Oof . . . eeww!'

Slayne burst into a faster run, swinging his cutlass in a circle. 'Damn kids, I hate 'em!' he shouted and threw his cutlass at Jim.

The cutlass curled through the air, twisting down straight towards Jim—

There was a swish of air and a snap of claws. Jolting the sword sideways, a mighty Rock Eagle flapped its huge wings and rose up, carrying the cutlass with it.

Jim skidded to a stop, his jaw open, watching the Rock Eagle fly out past the cliffs, Slayne's cutlass in its talons.

'Oi, stupid bird . . . give me my sword back!' The pirate shook his fist up at the bird soaring away over Seal Cove, the blade glinting in the moonlight. Once the Rock Eagle was out at sea, it opened its claws and the cutlass spiralled down through the air, vanishing into the ocean with barely a splash.

Slayne collapsed to his knees. 'No. No. Nooooo! My grandmama gave me that . . .' His huge sobs echoed across the night sky.

Meanwhile, Annie eyed Jim from the other side of the lawn.

He swerved away from the lighthouse door and down through the orchard. Knocking stinging nettles aside, he careened along the island's southern coastal path, towards the ship's mast where the Rigging Rats lived. With Annie on his heels, he ran across the sand dunes, through a clump of long grass and, feet squelching, into an expanse of muddy marshland.

'Yer gonna pay for this, boy!' Slayne bellowed. 'I loved that cutlass!'

Jim kept running.

Fffffftttttt-ssshhluurp.

The bog-fart rang in Jim's ears as he fought his way through the treacle-like mud, heart racing, turning to see Annie burst out of the grass. She pummelled her way across the marsh.

BANG!

Jim froze as a frightened chorus of bird screeches, frog croaks, monkey groans and insect whines rolled across the island.

'Enough!' Slayne yelled.

Jim turned round to see the pirate pointing the smoking barrel of a pistol up at the night sky.

The pirate captain lowered his flintlock pistol. A curl of white ground fog rolled silently over the marsh-land between Jim and Slayne.

'Give it up, boy,' the pirate growled. 'I ain't sailed 'alfway across the world for twelve bleedin' years for you to get away now!'

Jim's legs trembled, sinking deeper into the mud, his heart sinking too.

The only place it seemed he was going, was with these pirates.

CHAPTER TWENTY

SPLAT . . . SPLAT!

Two rotten cabbages smacked into the back of Slayne and Annie's heads, spraying eggy-smelling mould into the air, the two pirates falling face-first into the bog-mud.

Standing behind them was a smiling raccoon. Rafi winked at Jim. *'Run!'*

Jim tugged at his stuck legs, but they'd been sucked deep into the mud. He wiggled his body, until . . . *shh-hluuurrrrp* . . . he dragged one soil-slathered foot free and lunged forwards, pulling at his back leg.

Seeing thick bog-bubbles blowing out of the sides of Annie and Slayne's buried faces, Jim had a surge of strength and took more *shlurp* steps, his feet soon ten times bigger and heavier, coated in dripping bog-mud.

He looked ahead, through the ground mist, knowing the marshland ended *somewhere,* as two eyeballs flicked up out of the mud. They blinked, staring at Jim.

Jim raised one eyebrow.

The eyeballs were on stalks.

Bubbles rose out of the mud behind Cornelius, and popped.

Plip-parp.

'Oh, do excuse me,' said the crab, lifting a pincer out of the bog and clambering on to a patch of floating grass. Coated in black peat, the crab's shell looked almost invisible under his wobbly-white eyes. Cornelius glanced at the pirates as they climbed out of the sticky marsh, spitting brown bog-water out of their mouths. 'I say, old bean, in a bit of a bind, aren't you? No time to waste, eh? We *all* heard your cries and, as per usual, I am your humble—'

Parp.

'—messenger, here to say that jolly old Oskar advises you to head for the Turrets.' Cornelius winked. 'There's a good chap!'

'But, why . . . and how am I—'

Cornelius waved his pincer, as the bull-like bulk

165

of a mud-caked Annie Thache charged at Jim. The woman's face was a ball of rage and she stomped through the marsh like a swamp monster.

'Run along now . . . fast as you can!' Cornelius yelled. 'I'll hold them off.'

Parp.

Shhhluuurrrrp!

Jim yanked his leg free from the bog, stepped forward . . . and it hit solid ground. Wriggling his other leg free, he squelched up onto the brown, knobbly ground.

'Well, if I am honest,' Cornelius was yelling behind Jim, 'I may *not* hold them off. There are two of them and only one of me, and . . . with a wife and thirty-eight children to feed . . .'

Parp.

The ground shifted under Jim's feet. He looked down.

In the distance, Slayne was slapping and slurping his way across the swamp towards Jim, catching up with Annie.

'Don't underestimate an old pirate, yer scallywag!' Slayne growled, lifting up his mud-drenched flintlock pistol.

Cornelius clapped his claws together. 'Oh, how joyous, they *actually* use the word "scallywag" in real life!'

'Take another bleedin' step, boy, and I'll shoot!' Slayne sneered. 'You're comin' with me to . . . *pfft-pffft!* What the . . . *pffft-pffft* . . .' He looked up to the sky at hundreds of feathers spiralling down like pink rain in the moonlight. A flock of curved-beak birds from the Flaming Forest flamingo colony flew silently by overhead, each one shaking its body to release pink feathers. The pirate spat more feathers out of his mouth. 'How in thar . . . *pffft-pffft* . . . what is WRONG with this 'ere . . . *pffft-pffft* . . . ISLAND?'

Feathers covered Slayne and Annie, head-to-foot, sticking to the bog-slime on their hair, jackets and boots.

Jim smiled.

'What a flamboyance!' Cornelius clapped again. 'I'm sure you know that a group of flamingos is called a flamboyance, dear boy? Which is just, well, wonderful!' And with that, the crab disappeared under the mud.

Annie and Slayne stood, sinking in the bog, pulling

off clumps of feathers, looking like two scarecrows losing their stuffing. Then the pirates lifted their flint-lock pistols in unison, and pointed them at Jim.

'Stick yer bleedin' hands up, boy,' Slayne shouted. 'These stupid animals may want yer to stay, but ye ain't! I'm a-takin' yer back to your father, to get my reward!'

The ground under Jim's feet shunted sideways.

'I live here!' he yelled back, clenching a fist around the hilt of his cutlass. 'My family is *here*. I don't want to know my father. Especially if he's like *you*!'

Silence rolled across the misty swamp. Was that true? Did he really not want to know his father?

Slayne's laughter echoed across the island. 'You already know him better than yer think, lad!'

Clenching his teeth, Jim pulled the cutlass halfway out of its scabbard, glaring at the two pirates.

'Don't be an idiot, boy.'

Jim saw the darkness flick across Slayne's eyes. 'That parchment said that, if you harm me, you'll be fed to the sharks,' he said.

Slayne grunted. 'Think you're clever, don't-cha, eh?'

Annie glanced at Slayne. 'He has a point, cap'n, If you harm a hair on that boy's head, you'll live – or possibly *die* – to regret it.'

Jim's feet shifted again. Glancing down, he saw he was standing on a slimy brown knobbly lump, muddy bubbles rising to the bog's surface next to it. Each bubble *plipped* as they popped, leaving a faint whiff of cheese in the air.

Annie looked into Jim's eyes. 'If you give yourself

up, we'll treat you to a lovely hot meal and a nice, long ride on a pirate ship to a land far, far away from here.'

'I am *not* going with you. My home is here on this island!' Jim stamped his foot on the brown, knobbly ground. It groaned.

'Aside from that cutlass of yours, yer don't 'ave much experience with pirates.' Slayne's feet slurped forward in the marsh, getting closer and closer to Jim. 'We *are* a-takin' you, boy.' Slayne spat a flamingo feather off his nose, lowering his voice to a soft whisper. 'And as you've been here all alone on this 'orrible island for so long, running a stupid lighthouse by yerself, you'll be glad of some company. And a nice cuddle from yer father.' Slayne cackled.

Jim had heard enough. He tapped the knobbly lump beneath him three times, and Toad sprang out of the swamp slime with Jim balancing on top, spraying a wall of stinking mud at Slayne and Annie.

As Annie splashed down into the bog again, Slayne wobbled from the weight of mud, but managed to stay standing. Howling with rage as Jim bounded away on Toad, Slayne stretched out his arm holding the pistol.

Squinting one mud-stained eye down the barrel, he aimed it at Jim and pulled the trigger.

Pft-shlop.

Bog mud dribbled out of the gun's barrel, slapping down on to Slayne's feet. His eyes widened with fury.

'Aaaargh!' he yelled, throwing the pistol aside. 'Annie . . . GET 'IM . . . NOW!'

Clinging to Toad's slippery, warty back as he leapt away, Jim heard the pirate captain hollering in the distance.

'I said, get AFTER tha' godforsaken boy . . . and the . . . the giant frog he's escapin' on!'

'Mmph,' Annie spat out bog-water as she crawled to her feet. 'That was a *toad*, cap'n. Several species in the Caribbean Sea coastal areas grow—'

'I don't care . . . *GET AFTER 'IM!'*

CHAPTER TWENTY-ONE

Jim bounced up and forward, almost slipping off Toad's back as they bounded across the swamp.

'*Hold-ee on, weirdo!*' Toad kicked up rings of mud as he leapt onwards.

The horizon rose up, down, up, down as they leap-frogged – leap-*toaded* – out of the swamp. Slathered in slime and bog-water, Jim's stomach churning, Toad skidded to a stop through swirling grey ground mist in front of the jagged remnants of the island's Tumbledown Turrets. Jim shivered. With moonlight shining down on them, and the mist blanketing their bases, these ancient, abandoned fortress turrets looked like crumbling, rotten teeth from a giant's mouth.

Jim knew the island well, but these turrets creeped

him out. *Anything* could be staring down at you from their hidden tops, watching your every move.

Toad stomped towards the base of the first stone relic, wind swirling an eddy of ground mist out from where he stood. Jim slid off his back and landed on the wet grass, the mist curling back around him.

It was eerily quiet here. Except for the distant yells of the pursuing pirates.

'*Riiiibett-riiiibett!* Thwee lumps of cheese-a-reese for ride on Toad!' Toad blinked, clumps of bog-weed dripping off him.

Jim frowned. 'Um, I thought you were *saving* me?'

'Toad not save. Toad *need CHEEEESE!*' Toad slapped his webbed front foot on the ground.

Jim patted his hands over his muddy pockets, shrugging. 'Sorry, Toad, I don't have any.'

'Ugh. But Toad not had no cheese since . . . since,' Toad scratched his head, flicking slime across Jim's clothes, 'big, long time ago.'

'You mean,' Jim raised an eyebrow, 'since this morning when we gave you some to tell us which way the lantern thief had gone?'

Toad screwed up his face, thinking. 'Eh? Toad forget dis.' He closed his eyes tightly and, after a long silence, nodded. 'No, hang-diddly-on, ya-ha-ha, Toad 'member now! S'morning-a-ling. The beetle!'

'What . . . *WHAT*?' Jim poked a finger, hard, into a knobbly bit of Toad's skin. 'You *knew* the thief was a beetle *all along*?'

Toad nodded, slapping his webbed foot over his mouth, stifling a laugh behind it.

'I *cannot* believe this! You could have saved us so much—'

'Toad not save. Toad need cheese.' Toad burped

and this one smelt of twenty-year-old blue cheese fermented in sick.

Jim retched, clamping his hand over his nostrils. 'We gave you *all* the cheese we had this morning and you—'

'Yep. Big, long time ago now! Need CHEEEESE . . . for Toad ride!'

Jim huffed, kicking out at the swirling ground mist.

Two glowing green eyes appeared next to Toad's feet.

Jim grabbed the hilt of his sword.

Then Claudette slinked in front of Toad, dropped a huge lump of cheese on the ground before rubbing herself against Jim's legs and vanishing again.

'*Ssss-yes-nom-nom!*' Toad gobbled up the cheese, and – with a twisting flick of his huge, warty brown body – dived back into the mud.

'*Pssst! Pssssssssst! Over here!*'

Jim squinted up through the moonlit darkness. Scanning the swamp behind him, he saw two shadows through the mist. The pirates were catching up.

'*FOR GOODNESS' SAKE . . . PSSSSSSSST! OVER HERE!*'

Halfway up the first turret, on a jagged ledge, was Rafi's black and white face. The raccoon was waving frantically at Jim.

'RAFI!'

The raccoon slapped a paw on his furry forehead. *'Sssssh! Be QUIET . . . we've set a TRAP!'*

Jim held up one finger to his mouth, nodding, as he ran into a clearing, the turrets stretching above him.

Splip-splosh.

Something wet and freezing slapped onto the back of his neck and wriggled down his spine. Jim wiped it off his skin and saw a thick red-green goo that smelt of rotten tomatoes dribbling down his fingers.

He glanced up.

Instead of a starry night sky, above him hung a huge net full of foul-smelling, mouldy mangoes, putrid plums and decaying dragon fruit. Stretched out across four turrets, on either side of the clearing, the net drooped under the weight of decomposing oranges, melons, turnips, cabbages, apples and hundreds of black, squidgy banana skins.

'Oh.'

'Don't open your mouth when you look up!'

176

Tallulah squawked from the top of a turret.

Opposite Rafi, Oskar clung to some old railings. He leant over and slammed one long finger over his bulging orangutan lips. *'Sssssh.'*

Below him, stood Elsa, rocking side-to-side on her thick, grey legs. She nodded at Jim, smiling.

Jim whispered, 'Urgh, it stinks.'

'It be this bleedin' island tha' stinks, boy!' Slayne's gruff voice echoed across the clearing.

Jim spun round to see the two mud-and-pink-feather-caked pirates standing by the first turret.

Sssssshhhhhhiiiiiiiiiinnnnnnnggggggg.

Annie drew the cutlass from her belt. Glaring down the blade at Jim, her eyes were red-veined. 'No more games, little boy. Your time on this island . . . is up.'

Jim stared back down Annie's sword.

'Um, hello?' Slayne snatched Annie's cutlass from her hand. 'Give me tha', yer tired ole spinster! I'm the cap'n here, so I best 'ave the sword.' Slayne waved the cutlass in circles, striding forward. 'I be a-talkin' here, so you be a-listenin', lad. You're startin' to *upset* me.'

Jim bolted across the clearing to the turrets on its far side.

Wide-eyed, Slayne stomped his foot on the ground, glaring at Annie. 'Eh? See! Arrrr! What *is it* with kids? Why don't they listen to me?'

POING . . . POING . . . POING . . . POING!

The giant net's four ropes snapped.

Jim turned to see Slayne glance up a moment before a rancid waterfall of putrefied fruit and vegetables dropped on his and Annie's heads.

CHAPTER TWENTY-TWO

The tidal wave of wet, stinking, decaying food spread out to every side of the clearing; in the first blue rays of dawn's light, the area looked like a steaming mountain of lava.

Oskar swung across to the far turret using one of the net's broken ropes. Rafi scampered down from his ledge, mumbling about how much of *his* food they'd just wasted, and plucked a piece of slimy cabbage off the ground, shoving it into his mouth. He strolled across to the far turret too, with Elsa joining him, stamping through the food mound up to her knees. She curled Jim up in her trunk and lifted him into the air, plonking him on her back.

'There, dear, you're safe now.'

'I was saving those mouldy mangoes for my

birthday,' Rafi huffed.

Oskar hugged the raccoon. 'You made a great sacrifice for the island.'

Jim looked down at Oskar, from Elsa's back.

The orangutan stared up at him before grabbing Elsa's trunk to swing himself up beside Jim. 'I know we should have been more . . . honest with you. But, we had only one goal, Jim Rogers,' Oskar looked into Jim's eyes, 'to keep you safe.'

Jim thumped Elsa's back with his fist. 'I know that! But I'm angry with you for sheltering me for so long . . . it has put all of you in such danger!'

Oskar sucked in a sharp breath.

'How can I be worth so much trouble?' Jim's chest heaved. 'I don't want any of you to be hurt by these people because of me!'

'Not you – this is because of your father,' Elsa said gently.

Oskar considered what to say. 'If only you knew what joy you have brought us all, ever since you were a baby. We love you. That is why we have protected you. And why we will continue to protect you . . . for as long as we can.'

'Raaaaargh!'

Jim and the animals turned to see Captain Slayne rise out of the squelching food rubble, pointing his cutlass up at the dawn-lit sky. A chunk of pumpkin slipped off the end of his sword, smacking him on the head.

Annie spat her way up through the hunks of steaming food as Slayne glared at Jim, a gooey stream of pumpkin seeds sliding down his cheek.

'Yer know, I never did believe all thar stories people told me about this bleedin' island. That it were haunted; that ships a-goin' anywhere near it were *always* wrecked; that the island turned *invisible* somehow; an tha', during storms, the souls of dead sailors walked on the water out by Black Eel Rock, like slack-jawed ghosts.'

The pirate waded forward through the food mound, Annie following.

'Bein' a pirate an' all, I know we like to embellish a good sea story. It makes us seem scarier. But I 'ave to say, Jim lad, this island's got some a-different kind of secrets up its sleeves, ain't it? That damn lighthouse 'an you lot . . . how in thar name of Neptune are yer a-gettin' these animals to do yer biddin', boy?' The captain scratched his food-slimed head. 'From where I'm standin', I can see more – lots more – pretty pennies on the horizon.' Slayne turned to Annie. 'Can ye imagine it – a performin' monkey, a giant elephant what does tricks, maybe a dancin' raccoon, and—'

'I am an orangutan, you idiot,' Oskar said, swinging off Elsa's back and landing in front of the pirate.

Slayne's jaw dropped.

'Pardon-what-come-again? What-in-the-blazes-did-yer . . . yer . . .' Slayne stammered, dropping his cutlass. 'Did you . . . did you . . . just . . .' He turned to Annie again. 'Did you . . . did . . . er, I mean, did you just hear wha' that monkey—'

Oskar sighed. 'Orangutan.'

'Do any of you intend on eating this food?' Rafi said, munching on some slithery cucumber.

'What? WHAT?' Slayne shook his head. 'The raccoon talks *too*? What dark magic is this?'

'We *all* speak on this island, dear, albeit some of us in our own languages.' Elsa lifted her trunk to the side of her head and saluted. 'Jim doesn't order us to do anything. We are all equal on Lighthouse Island. And he belongs here, with his island family. Not with *you*, or anyone else. You will not be breaking our family up,' Elsa narrowed her eyes at Slayne, *'dear.'*

Slayne swallowed. 'Did these animals . . . 'ave they . . . did you *grow up* with 'em all?'

Jim nodded. And, in that moment, he realised the animals, his *friends*, were surprising to Slayne and Annie. That they must be different to animals in the world beyond.

183

Jim glared down at Slayne, shivering, as he saw a new, hungry look in the pirate's eyes. A look that told him his friends were in even more danger than he'd thought. 'These animals are my family. Get back on your ship, sail away and forget you ever stepped foot on our island.'

Annie laughed. 'That's *funny*, after all we've been through to find you!' She stepped towards Rafi, tilting her head to one side, staring at him. 'I remember, when my brother, our commander, was young, he told us tales of talking animals on a faraway island. But we all thought he was daydreaming. Or that he'd drunk too much rum.' She turned to look at Jim. 'Come with us, Jim. Come meet him. Surely you want to meet your real father?'

'I may have been born like you and your *brother*, my father,' Jim hissed, 'but it doesn't mean I want to be like you.'

Annie smiled. 'But, if you come with us, there are things in the human world – your world – you could have that are beyond any of the dreams you have on this tiny island.'

Slayne's shrill cackle sliced across the clearing.

'Save yer fancy breath, woman. He's comin' with us,

whether he likes it or not.' Slayne glared up at Jim. 'You, lad, an' all these *freaks of nature*, and yer stupid lighthouse . . . y'are all mine. I'm gonna make a bleedin' fortune.' Slayne's voice was frighteningly high-pitched now. 'A fortune, I tell you! Annie, let's get 'em! All of 'em!'

Annie glanced at him, then at all the animals, especially the huge elephant. 'Maybe we should wait for the rest of the crew to—'

Slayne raised his cutlass and charged at Jim and the animals.

Trumpeting a scream, Elsa leapt sideways, wrapped her trunk around Rafi and plonked the raccoon on her back behind Jim. Tallulah rose into the air and landed on one of Elsa's tusks as Oskar swung back up, gripping the raccoon's shoulders. The elephant pounded away through the crumbling turrets and into the swirling mist.

Roaring as he slid in the rotten food, Slayne ran full pelt after them.

Annie sighed, watching her captain disappear through the mist. She wiped some putrid plum mush off her face and ran after them all.

CHAPTER TWENTY-THREE

Bursting out from between two palm trees, Elsa thundered out of the Flaming Forest and onto the island's east coast beach.

An orange sunrise peered over the horizon, spraying the sea with a glassy line of fish-scale lights as the elephant skidded across the sand.

Jim crouched forward, gripping Elsa's ears as she picked up speed.

Elsa ran through a flock of flamingos and hundreds of them exploded into flight. A wall of pink birds surged all around Jim, Elsa, Tallulah, Rafi and Oskar, blocking out the sunrise, the *clack-clack-clack* of beating wings rolling through Jim's ears.

'Sorry, my friends!' Elsa bellowed, out of breath, as she pummelled along the beach, a comet tail of sand spraying up behind her.

As the last batch of flamingos flew upwards, Jim and the animals saw what had been hiding behind them.

The pirate ship.

The ship they had saved from Black Eel Rock and watched sail away from their island was now sitting in shallow, mauve-clear water, near the beach. Silhouetted in black, against the rising sun, the ship's sails flapped in the breeze, beckoning Jim and the animals towards it.

Elsa snorted, digging her heels into the sand and sliding to a stop.

'That ship never left the bay, it sailed around the island!' Rafi gasped. 'This is bad. So, so bad. How many more of them are there?'

Oskar growled. 'We must think of a plan to stop them taking Jim and make them leave the island.'

'This is all my fault,' Jim cried. 'If I had never arrived on this island—'

Elsa lifted her trunk up, patting Jim on the head. 'Don't say such things, dear. As Oskar said, you coming here was the best thing that's happened to all of us! We won't let these people take you away.'

'Wouldn't it be easier if I gave myself up?' Jim slid down Elsa's flank and landed with a thud on the sand. 'The pirates want *me*. For the reward from my father. Maybe they would leave you all alone if they had me?'

Oskar swung down Elsa's trunk, landing in front of Jim. 'You are mistaken. Human people are greedy. They always want more.' The orangutan shook his head gravely. 'I have seen what men are capable of. Now they know we are here, taking you will only be the start of it.'

Jim and the animals all turned as an orange light flashed within the ship's silhouette. A long, dark shadow shot out from the ship and across the sea.

'What—?'

BOOM! Flummmmpppffffff-sssssshhhh!

Sand sprayed into the air a few feet ahead of Jim, hitting him in the face. The shockwave knocked him sideways, and he rolled across the sand, into the water, escaping the rumbling ground. Drenched, he leapt up and ran back to where Oskar was gripping one of Elsa's sturdy legs. Rafi held on to another, and Tallulah was flying around, cawing and trembling.

'What was *that*?' Jim scrambled over to Oskar, sitting against Elsa's leg and looking at the top of a curved, steaming chunk of metal buried in the sand.

'*That*, Jim, was a cannonball . . .' Another spark of orange light flickered inside the ship's dark shape. Then another, and another. 'And there are more coming, so we must *RUN!*'

A long, black cannonball shadow painted a trail over the sea, heading their way. Jim bolted out from behind Elsa's legs and across the beach towards the trees.

BOOM! Flummmmpppffffff-ssssssshhhh!

A second wall of exploding sand smacked Jim's body so hard he flew, like loose seaweed in a tide, across the beach. Legs flipping up, around and upside down, he tumbled through the air, head-first, towards the sand and—

He was wrenched sideways as Elsa swiped him out of the air and put him on her back. Oskar leapt up too, the elephant picking up Rafi and heading for cover by the line of Flaming Forest trees. Jim's head spun as the top of a palm tree exploded into flames, fronds and bark spitting across the beach, just missing them.

'Why are they shooting these balls of fire at us?' Jim yelled at Oskar, who was gripping Elsa's ears. Rafi clung to the orangutan with one arm, the other held over his eyes, as Jim bounced up and down. 'I thought they wanted to take me alive!'

'The minds of people, especially pirates, are neither sharp nor straightforward.' Oskar pointed a long, orange-haired arm at the forest. 'There is a path through the trees farther up the beach . . . keep going, Elsa!'

Elsa grunted, lowered her head and thumped her

legs harder, faster over the sand.

The break in the foliage was up ahead, but Jim saw the ship's silhouette burst with another flash of light. 'More cannonballs!'

Elsa trumpeted, surging onwards along the beach, the new cannonball splitting a trench in the sea as it flew just above the water.

'*Turn down the path, Elsa, TURN!*' Jim's knuckles were white as he gripped her flanks.

'*All right, dear!*' She stamped her right front leg into the sand, skidding, and her rear legs juddered sideways until her huge body pointed at the tree line.

BOOM!

Flummmmpppffffff-sssssshhhh!

The cannonball hit the sand next to Elsa.

The elephant roared as she rolled into the air. Oskar and Rafi flew off her back, their arms pin-wheeling, and Jim was catapulted across the tree line. With air punched out of his lungs, Jim grabbed out at leaves as he smashed down through mangrove trees, before thudding into a thistle bush.

'Urgh . . . *ooowww!*' Jumping straight up, he ran back to the beach, his body aching.

Elsa was already on her feet and Rafi was brushing sand out of Oskar's hair.

'This is stupid.' Jim stormed over to Oskar, grabbing the hilt of his cutlass. 'If I don't give myself up, we're all going to be killed!'

Oskar batted Rafi's paws off him, glaring at Jim. 'Listen to me. I have devoted my *life*, as has every other animal on this island, to bringing you up. To sheltering you from . . . *them*. From *him* who seeks you.'

Jim opened his mouth.

Oskar raised one long finger in the air. 'I *will not* let you sacrifice all that just to try and . . . *and* . . . I *cannot* . . .'

Jim clenched his jaw as tears swelled in his friend's eyes. 'But perhaps . . . perhaps it is *time* for me to leave the island? Perhaps Captain Slayne . . .'

Jim's heart thumped as Oskar looked down, away from him. He heard Elsa sigh, wiping a tear from one of her eyes with her trunk.

Rafi punched Jim on the arm. '*This* is your home, dimwit!'

Jim's face flushed hot as he held out his arms and went towards Oskar to—

The tip of a cutlass blade slid out of the shadows, in between Oskar and Jim, and Captain Slayne emerged from the tree line.

'Oh, so *sorry*,' the pirate mocked, 'did I interrupt a tender moment?'

Annie broke through the foliage beside him, gasping for breath.

Jim gripped his cutlass' hilt as Slayne leant closer to him, sneering. 'Y'are nuthin' more than a beast yerself, are ye, boy?'

Jim drew his sword, brown flakes of rust sprinkling on to the sand, and swiped it through the air. 'Let the animals go and I'll . . . I'll . . .'

'You'll *what*, lad?' Slayne spat a laugh. 'Where d'yer think you got tha blade of yours from, eh?' A twinkle flicked across Slayne's dark eyes. 'Yer father had tha thar sword when he was escapin' the island of Nassau with you and his wife, your mother. That were before he got cornered by Nassau's pirate-huntin' governor, Woodes Rogers, and his men. He was captured, for a while, but yer mother . . . not her. Ha! She snatched the cutlass and, bein' pretty handy with it, she got away long enough to shove you and the sword in a barrel o'

193

rum and set yer out to sea.' Slayne licked his lips. 'To keep yer from bein' taken prisoner, boy. To keep yer from a life you would *never* have survived.'

Sweat broke out on Jim's forehead.

'Yer mother put a note in that rum barrel too, with your name on it. She told me so. And the sly one tha' she be, she wrote your name as Jim Rogers – givin' you the governor's surname – as she figured you'd be safer with that one, than with your *real* name.'

Jim looked at Oskar. The orangutan's eyes were full of sadness.

'Who *is* my father?'

Slayne glanced over at Annie.

'As I told you, he's my brother,' she narrowed her eyes at Jim, 'and you might know him as Edward. Edward Thache. He's given himself many names over the years . . . Edward Teach, Edward Thatch. But now he's all grown up, and is the scourge of the Caribbean Sea, we call him Blackbeard.'

Oskar stumbled backwards, turning to Annie. 'You lie! The Edward we knew when he came here was—'

'A good man?' Annie nodded sullenly. 'Oh, he used to be.'

'The hearts o' men change, and never fer the better,' Slayne chuckled. 'So, there y'are, lad, you're the son of the Pirate King!'

Jim shook his head, looking at the animals, his mind spinning. He stumbled sideways, tears in his eyes, as Slayne's words thudded into his head. How could helpful Edward . . . the kindly shipwrecked sailor the animals loved be . . .

Jim closed his eyes to stop the sand, animals and people whirling around him. But all he saw across the back of his eyelids were Elsa's paintings of Edward at the lighthouse. In them, Edward's smiling face was melting, twisting into a snarling old man . . . into . . . *his father*.

Annie seized her moment and snatched Jim up off the beach, throwing him over her shoulder.

Elsa snorted and wrapped her trunk around Slayne's neck, lifting him up into the air. 'You are a *very* nasty little man, aren't you, dear?'

His face flooding red, Slayne spluttered, clawing at Elsa's trunk.

Jim kicked at Annie, before he called to the elephant, 'It's all right, Elsa, let him go.'

Elsa glared at Jim, her nostrils flaring, before she slowly opened her trunk and let Slayne roll out, hitting the beach hard.

Annie shoved past Rafi, Oskar and Tallulah to haul Slayne up, Jim writhing on her back, hanging upside-down over her shoulder.

Slayne grinned at the animals, staring at them all in turn. Then he spat on the sand in front of them.

The animals watched helplessly as the pirates dragged Jim along the beach, into the distance, towards their ship.

CHAPTER TWENTY-FOUR

A sharp pain shot through Jim's knees as Annie pushed him down on the ship's deck. He crawled away, over to the base of a wooden mast, backing up against it. Looking around, he took in the huge, wooden expanse of the pirate ship. There were metal grills in the deck floor; lanterns hanging from steps up to a wide, curved quarterdeck; ropes, buckets and piles of cannonballs lying scattered around; and the overwhelming smell of frying onions and cooking meat wafting up from somewhere below.

And groups of bedraggled, gap-toothed men standing around, staring at him.

Jim's fingers and toes fizzed with pins and needles, his chest was tight too. This was the first time he had ever left the island.

'What's thar matter, beast-boy?' Slayne stomped over, standing above him. 'Missin' yer aberration-friends already?' Slayne turned and waved at the crew, then pointed down at Jim. 'Look here, men . . . we finally got ourselves the snivellin' brat who's gonna make us RICH!'

The crew punched the air, roaring.

Jim's whole body shook, and he jumped when a huge, bald man with tattoos and earrings threw a wet rag at him.

'Got a long journey ahead, make yerself useful.'

Jim pulled the cloth off his face and, despite his knotted stomach, he slid his back up the mast to stand opposite a sneering Slayne.

The ship's sails flapped in the wind, the deck shunting sideways as they began sailing away from the beach, out to sea.

'I don't work for you,' Jim hissed, screwing up the rag. He leant up on tiptoes and stuffed it into Captain Slayne's mouth.

The pirate's eyes widened in fury, and the whole crew fell silent.

Slayne spat the cloth out, his nostrils flaring. 'Yer

gonna regret that, boy.' The pirate captain turned and clicked his fingers at his quartermaster, Annie. 'Take 'im to the brig. The nasty one tha' the men use as a latrine.'

'Come on, Cap'n,' Annie protested. 'He's displaying all the qualities of a good pirate. His father will be *proud*. Should we punish him for—'

'Don't argue with me!' The pirate's face turned blood red. 'He may be Blackbeard's son, but this is my ship and the boy's a flippin' animal . . . so we shall a-treat 'im as such!'

Annie ripped Jim from the mast and marched him across deck.

The ship juddered again, and he and Annie slid sideways as the crew hoisted sails, wound-up ropes, and carried cannonballs below deck. Jim glared up at Annie, wriggling against her grip, and the quarter-master gave him an apologetic half-smile as she kicked open a door underneath the quarterdeck. The rancid, hot stench of old urine filled Jim's nose, and the chilly darkness inside the brig reached out to him.

Annie pushed him inside.

'If I were you, I'd keep your head down,' she said,

glancing back across the deck at Slayne.

'Is this . . . how the world beyond treats human boys?' Jim whispered. 'Will I be kept in here the whole journey?'

Annie spat an empty chuckle. 'You have no idea, do you?' She leant forward, snatching Jim's chin and cheeks in one hand, squeezing them. 'You're a fresh-faced young lad, right now, Jim. But that won't last.' She pointed out at the ship's skinny crew, all shuffling around deck as if half-dead. 'Look at them. Worn out. Bitter. Beaten. That's what life at sea is. And Slayne's ship, here . . . this is luxury. Wait till your father shows you a real pirate's life.'

Annie slammed the door shut in Jim's face.

A lock clunked and darkness took over; the kind of solid darkness that presses on your skin. No stars in it. No clifftop view with a lighthouse sweeping its one, two, three . . . three-and-a-half beams across the ocean. Just the smell of dust, wood, sea, fish and urine.

Jim knew he was nothing to these pirates. Just a means to get rich. He should have listened to Oskar . . . to all the animals, and fought harder to not leave his home.

'I only wanted to save them,' he whispered into the darkness. But that wasn't entirely true. He had wanted to know a little of the world, and his father.

Slayne was yelling orders at his men outside, then the ship rolled sideways. Jim held out his arms to stay balanced, not that he could tell which way was up, down, left or right in this blackness. It was so dark in here he couldn't feel time passing. Being outside on the island, seeing the sun, the dawn, the dusk, he always *knew* where he was and what time it was.

He shook his head. 'Come on!'

After years living in his tiny, hidden ceiling room, surely this brig was bearable . . .

But, no. The darkness was already pressing on his mind.

He wondered what the animals were doing without him. Were they missing him? He pulled in a breath, feeling like he was sucking in the darkness.

He shivered and tried to picture the comforting beams of his lighthouse home.

Sssssh-thump.

Jim jumped. He must have fallen asleep for a

moment. Or had it been hours?

Sssssh-thump.

Glancing to where he thought the sound had come from, he squinted. But it was useless, he couldn't see anything.

Sssssh-thump.

He spun round in another direction – had the sound come from over *there*?

'Who . . . who's there?'

Sssssh-thump.

'Owa-ch!' A sharp, throbbing pain shot through Jim's big toe. He yanked his foot out from under the heavy object that had landed on it. 'Who are you? Show yourself!'

A muffled fizzing sound. Then a small light flickered to life inside a lantern laying on the floor.

Jim's eyes went blurry from the bright flame, before the tiny, furry shape it lit up came into focus.

'Flum!' Jim yelled, dropping to his knees and scooping the Rigging Rat up in his hand. He hugged the little rat hard. 'Oh, I'm so pleased to see you!'

Flum wriggled free, chittering away, and leapt down next to the lantern again, pointing frantically to

Jim's foot. Next to it, lying on the floor, was the object Flum had dropped on his toe: an axe.

'How did you . . . where did you . . . ?' Jim picked up the axe, twirling it around in his hand, his body swaying as the ship rolled over some big waves. 'Where are Rum and Sum?'

Flum stood up on his hind legs and scratched his head. Chittering as he considered something, the rat finally jumped onto the axe handle, pretending to lift it whilst pointing at Jim. Flum swung his body into a sideways chopping motion, looking up at the brig ceiling as if he was miming slicing something very tall. Then the rat grabbed his tail in one paw, wrapped it around his own leg, collapsed on his side and poked his tongue out of his mouth. Then he flipped himself upside down, his back legs up in the air.

Jim raised his eyebrows as Flum continued to act out running around, throwing imaginary objects and miming chopping motions. Finally, Flum looked at Jim and bounced up and down excitedly.

Jim stared at him. 'I *wish* I spoke rat.'

Ignoring Jim's bemused expression, Flum clapped and chittered happily, running up Jim's leg, across his chest and sitting on his shoulder.

'What do I need to do first?' he asked, glancing at the rat, but Flum was already pointing at the door, making chopping motions again with his front feet.

Hands quivering, Jim snatched up the lamp and held it to the crack in the door. After a moment of spinning, stomach-in-throat nausea from the ship's rolling motion, he bent closer and squinted through the lamp flame. He saw the metal bolt on the other side was straight – a flat iron bar had been dropped into a slot either side of the wooden doorframe, securing it. The rat made more frantic chopping motions but he was miming each chop *upwards.*

Jim put down the lamp, dragged his feet apart and swung the axe back between his legs. Counting under his breath, on three he yanked the axe up, hard.

KRANG!

The metal bar outside the door shunted up and then crashed back down into its holding.

Jim swung the axe up again, harder and faster this time.

KRANG . . . CLANK!

The door swung gently open, creaking.

Flum jumped up and down on Jim's shoulder, pumping his little claws in the air.

Jim mouthed a silent *'YES!'*, pushing the door open and stepping over the metal bar on the floor. Crouching down, Jim scanned the deck stretching ahead. The ship was lurching at odd, head-spinning angles and it was almost as dark out here as it had been inside the brig. Glancing up through the masts, rigging and sails he saw the moon lighting the night sky. Jim's heart sank. How long had they been sailing? The island must be long gone in the distance by now.

Footsteps.

Jim hid behind the post outside the brig. To his left, two feet ran down the steps from the quarterdeck and Jim watched as a man joined several others near the ship's portside railings. The pirates raised tankards into the air, cackled and drank.

Perhaps none of them had heard him break out of the brig.

'What now?' he whispered to Flum.

The rat jabbed his claw towards the crewmen.

Jim frowned. *'I can't fight all of them!'*

Flum shook his head, pointing downwards.

Peering around the post, Jim looked across at the men, his eyes widening. Weaving in and out of the pirates' legs, with two rope ends held in their rat teeth, were Rum and Sum. Rum twisted his rope round one way, and Sum twisted his rope round the opposite way. The men's legs were quickly intertwined, but they kept laughing and drinking, unaware of what was happening at their feet.

The two rats scampered across deck with the rope ends in their mouths and leapt onto the main mast, clawing their way up, ropes trailing behind them.

Now his eyes had adjusted to the moonlight and he saw lots of ropes snaking across the deck. Some curled down the grating, disappearing below deck, others wound their way up the quarterdeck. Jim's two nimble Rigging Rat friends climbed the mast, traversing the sails and winding the two ropes around the rigging netting and the top horizontal separators.

Flum bounced up and down on his shoulder, squeaking, pointing to the main mast.

'What? I can't go out there,' he whispered, staying pressed up against the post. 'Those pirates will throw me back in the brig!'

Flum rolled his eyes and pointed a stern paw out to the main mast.

'All right,' he huffed. 'But what am I doing when I get there?'

Flum swung his little arms hard, once, staring at the axe.

'You seriously want me to CHOP the mast down?' He glanced down at the axe in his hand, wide-eyed. Was Flum serious? Then, looking at the ropes snaking around on deck, he thought about the rat's mime in the brig. It was a *rope* Flum wanted him to chop!

A beam of light shot across the bow of the ship, lighting up the sails, darkening the night sky behind them. Then another beam swept across. Another. And then a dimmer one.

The lighthouse!

CHAPTER TWENTY-FIVE

With no time to lose, Jim burst out from behind the post, running across deck, axe in hand.

The lighthouse beams lit up the ship's masts, sails, quarterdeck and him running.

'PRISONER ESCAPE!' someone yelled, and the crewmen drinking by the railings all swivelled round, glaring at him. Growling, they threw their tankards aside and drew their cutlasses, leaping forward . . .

. . . and all of them tripped on the ropes around their ankles.

Collapsing on top of one another, the pirates rolled around, cutlasses flying in all directions. There were groans, shoves and then the men started punching one another, trying to wriggle their legs free.

Jim was at the mast now, and swung the axe straight

at it, chunks of wood flying across deck. He wrenched the embedded axe out, slicing it into the mast again before realising there were no ropes to chop.

'SOMEONE STOP THAT BOY!' a sharp voice yelled from up by the ship's wheel. Slayne.

Footsteps and roaring, everywhere now; yelling, jostling men springing from all parts of the ship.

Pirates were running at Jim along the dark deck, but he saw ropes tied to every single one of their ankles. The rats had been busy.

Palms sweating, Jim yanked the axe blade loose from the mast, splinters flying past his face.

Flum leapt off Jim's shoulder onto the mast to grab in his mouth one of the lower ends of the two taut ropes that Rum and Sum had carried up the rigging. Flum crawled around the mast, dragging the rope in front of Jim as he smashed the axe blade at it again and—

TWOING!

—the rope sliced in half and sprang upwards in a whipping arc, at such speed Jim felt the wind-trail from it just miss his face. The snapped rope end disappeared above and, after a moment, the second rope slammed tight against the mast, creaking as it rubbed against the wood, wisps of friction-smoke swirling into the air.

Rum and Sum leapt from the mast, tumbling down onto Jim's shoulder, next to their brother. Chittering to one another, and hugging, they looked up as a loud metallic *CLANK* ripped across the ship.

The lighthouse beams lit up the broken, whipping rope as it surged through pulley after pulley, so fast it snapped them from their holdings, the rope slicing through sails and nets, splitting them apart like a fifty-foot thrashing blade.

Then the rigging dropped.

Jim gasped as the mast's top sail snapped loose and flew out into the ocean, like a dying giant moth, at the same time as the wooden spar pole it had been fastened to hammered down into the next pole below it. Then the next. Sails, nets, rigging, ropes, pulleys and huge, heavy spar poles smashed their way down the mast towards the deck.

Jim dropped the axe and ran.

Slayne swung his cutlass at Jim's head, but he ducked, changing course to head for the quarterdeck steps. Slayne spun round, yelling something at his

men, and was about to swipe his cutlass at Jim again
. . . when he was whipped sideways off the steps, his
left leg shooting out and above him as he was swung
upside down across the length of the deck.

The twisted mess of rigging and sails hit the deck in
a crescendo of jagged edges and chaotic noise, and Jim
turned to see pirate after pirate snatched off their feet
and pulled up into the air.

The deck went deathly quiet except for the creaking of many ropes, as the lighthouse beams soared
across and lit up a pirate ship with *all* its pirates hanging upside down, gently swinging from the rigging
separators.

Jim laughed.

Rum, Flum and Sum high-fived each other.

'Boy!' Slayne swung back and forth the length of
the whole ship, his two-beards dangling like limp
sausages over his face. He glared at Jim every time he
swung by above him. 'Get me down . . . NOW!'

'Sorry, Captain,' Jim smiled, 'I'd love to, but I don't
have time to *hang around*.'

Rum, Flum and Sum chittered with laughter on his
shoulder.

'There's no bleedin'
way you're escapin', boy!'
Slayne yelled. The pirate
pulled his cutlass upwards, as he
swung upside down, and started slicing away at the
rope hanging above his foot. 'We're on the ocean now,
you ain't a-goin' NOWHERE!'

Annie swung past Slayne, with her long hair
dangling down. 'I told you this boy would be a force to
reckon with, he's his father's son.'

The pirate wriggled around as he cut at his

213

rope. 'Why . . . why . . . *WHY* are yer NEVER supportive of me?'

Annie rolled her eyes.

As the pirates argued, the three Rigging Rats climbed on top of one another on Jim's shoulder, all pointing outwards in four different directions – Rum pointed up at the sky; in the middle, Flum held out his little arms in opposite directions; and at the bottom Sum stood on one leg, pointing his other leg down at the deck.

Jim frowned, peering in all the directions the rats were pointing. 'Are you . . . a *compass*?'

The rats jumped up and down, gesturing frantically, and Jim looked up at the sky to see a lighthouse beam sweep across the ship from east to west. Jim gulped. They weren't far away from his island home after all. Beam three-and-half's sea-mirage vanishing trick had confused the crew whilst he'd been in the brig. The ship must have been sailing in circles for hours and was now . . .

A beam lit up a black, sharp-toothed mouth next to the ship's starboard side.

Jim froze, the air going so cold it chilled his lungs.

Shaking, he looked into a huge, jagged eye. And, as the lighthouse beam lingered on it, the eye gleamed, alive, staring straight at him. The beam moved on and, in the moonlit darkness, Jim saw the long, ragged length of Black Eel Rock stretching out beside the ship, as if it were swimming alongside it.

About to hit it.

Jim leapt off the quarterdeck steps, running underneath the hanging pirates, all of them swiping at him. But he ducked and weaved, passing under Captain Slayne as the pirate continued sawing at his rope. Jim ran up to the ship's wheel, grabbed the wooden spokes and, with three rats chittering in his ear, he tugged the wheel port side because, no matter what these people had done, he couldn't let them be shipwrecked.

The wheel rumbled round and, in no time, the ship turned hard right, away from Black Eel Rock, the monster rock's eye sinking away into the ocean darkness as the ship's bow ploughed into deeper water.

Jim sighed with relief, leapt from the wheel and slid down the wooden bannister. Running across deck, with his three Rigging Rat friends on his shoulder, he clambered up onto the ship's port-side railings. It was time to swim home. The sea wind whipped his hair sideways and he turned back to see Slayne stomping towards him.

'Yer'll never make it from 'ere, boy, don't be stupid!'

Jim glanced down at the churning, surging dark water below. Rum, Flum and Sum clutched one another, shaking, and he grit his teeth at Slayne. 'I don't see the world the same way as you do, Captain.'

Slayne slid to a stop, his cutlass dropping down beside his leg.

Jim glared at him, gripping the railings as the wind lashed his body.

'If you jump, this won't be the end!' Slayne howled, narrowing his eyes. Annie limped across deck to join him, a length of sliced rope trailing at her ankle. 'Yer'll see me again, lad,' the pirate captain yelled over the roiling sea. 'And, when you do, I promise . . . I'll bring the gates of hell to yer pretty little island!'

Jim stroked the three rats gently, looking away from Slayne's incandescent face and, with the lighthouse beams shining in the distance, vanishing the island from view with their sea-mirage deceit, Jim leapt off the ship's side and—

Sharp pain ripped across his neck as *something* clamped around it, yanking him and the rats back up to be flung down on deck. Spluttering, head spinning, the Rigging Rats tumbling off his shoulder and scampering up onto the railings, Jim slowly lifted his face off the deck, blinking at the two muddy black boots standing next to his head, towering above him.

A shiver of cold shot through him.

Jim scrambled to his feet in front of a tall, wide man in charcoal-black breeches, long overcoat and dark shirt with a large, scrawny raven sitting on his shoulder. Two pistols were strapped to belts across his chest, the man's eyes were hollow pits inside a scarred face, and his beard was as black as night.

'Hello, my boy,' he said, his voice like broken glass.

'You're . . . you're . . .' stammered Jim.

The man nodded, suddenly yanking a cutlass out from under his overcoat and slamming it down on the railing near the rats. Splinters of wood flew into the air. 'Vermin.' He swiped the cutlass down again, just missing Rum's tail. And sliced again, a whisker's breadth from Sum's nose.

'Stop it!' Jim kicked the man in the shin.

The jet black raven on the man's shoulder screeched down at Jim as the man turned and jabbed the cutlass at him.

'Soft spot for *vermin*, have you? Like you have for all those other . . . animals.'

The man smiled, the twisted white tissue of his scars expanding like calcified worms on his face. 'Huge apologies for not joining you earlier, my boy.' The black-clad man squeezed the end of his beard, thinking. 'Actually, I'm not sorry.' He grabbed Jim by the scruff of his shirt and stomped across deck with him, slamming Jim up against the smashed remains of a mast. The man rummaged in his jacket, flicked open a piece of old parchment and, leaning over Jim, pulled a dagger from his belt. He drew the blade back above his shoulder and stabbed it straight down . . .

. . . through the poster, into the mast above Jim's head.

Heart pounding, Jim looked up to see the word 'WANTED' and the sketch of him as a baby in a barrel, fluttering in the sea breeze, the paper whipping against his forehead.

Blackbeard pushed his mouth, slowly, up against Jim's ear and whispered, 'You're mine again now, boy.'

CHAPTER TWENTY-SIX

The creaking of swinging, upside-down-pirate ropes rang in Jim's ears, along with the smash of waves against the ship's hull. The parchment smacked him in the face as his father's hot, rum-soaked breath made him wince.

'Get . . . off . . . me!'

Blackbeard sneered. 'That's my boy, *there* you are.' The pirate sniffed the top of Jim's head, breathing him in, before ripping Jim off the broken mast and pushing him out to the middle of the deck.

Looking around, Jim heard thudding, shuffling sounds to his right and knew some of the hanging pirates were breaking free.

'You must understand,' Blackbeard snarled, his knotted scars twitching, 'I have hunted high and low

219

for you, for years. Sent armies of men out looking for you. Because . . . I need you. And, although you don't see it yet, you need me.'

'What for?' Jim scowled.

'I have amassed a great following of pirates, boy, and they admire me. They'll do *anything* for me.' Blackbeard's mouth twisted into an empty half-smile. 'But we need a new—'

Jim bolted towards the quarterdeck, but skidded to a stop in front of Slayne and Annie as they stepped out

of the shadows. Slayne lashed out at Jim, but he leapt backwards . . . and hit the black wall of his father's overcoat.

'No one is coming for you, boy,' Blackbeard whispered. The hairs of the pirate's beard scratched the back of Jim's neck. 'You belong to me. Embrace your destiny: you're a pirate, like me. Like Annie here. Like all of us.'

Jim wriggled from his father's clutches, glaring at Slayne and Annie, and then turning back to Blackbeard. Looking around for the rats, he couldn't see them.

He was on his own.

Blackbeard lifted his cutlass, the blade glinting in the moonlight, and pointed it at Jim. 'As I was saying, boy, you're the heir to a pirate kingdom and you *will* come with me.'

Jim narrowed his eyes at Blackbeard and slowly shook his head.

Blackbeard roared. 'I'm not making myself clear enough, boy. If I can't have you, then no one will.'

Annie stepped forward, holding out a fist with three rats' tails clenched in it. Dangling upside down, wriggling crazily, were Rum, Flum and Sum.

'See how much *they* like it!' she said.

Blackbeard smiled, nodded at Jim and then flicked his cutlass up into the air. Snatching at the blade-end, he flipped it round and held the hilt out towards Jim. 'Here, show me how much of a pirate you already are, Jim Thache. Kill the vermin.'

Jim glanced at the three quivering rats, at Annie's face, then back at the sword.

'No!'

The cracked squeaks of his rat friends tore at Jim's heart. Rum, Flum and Sum clung to one another.

Jim closed his eyes before slowly reaching out to grasp the cutlass' hilt.

'That's it, my son,' the pirate said, 'prove you're a man!'

The raven squawked from Blackbeard's shoulder as Jim gripped the cutlass, sweat dripping off his forehead. 'I'm ... I ...'

'Do it, boy.' The pirate shoved Jim towards the huddled-together rats. 'I know you've been desperate to know me. But the only way to know *me*, boy, is to know yourself. Your true self.'

Jim stepped towards the Rigging Rats, the cutlass

shaking in his hand, the rats cowering from him. The creaking of the hanging pirate ropes holding the skinny, dead-eyed crew, grew louder again. The ocean screamed out below, and the sea-stained, bedraggled ship closed in on him.

'You can learn from me, Jim.' Blackbeard's top lip twitched. 'Learn to be *more* than a boy on a lost island. I want you to become my successor, you will make a fine—'

Jim ran at Annie, knocking her sideways with a spinning air-kick, the three Rigging Rats flying across the deck.

Skidding over the boards, Jim slid the cutlass blade, flat, along the deck railings, the rats scurrying up it, onto his shoulder. He swerved to face his father. 'These *vermin* are my friends. And I'll give the "lessons" a miss, thanks, father.'

Blackbeard's hollow eyes blazed as he ran at Jim.

Jim leapt up on to the quarterdeck's steps as his father snatched Slayne's cutlass from his hand, swinging it at Jim's legs. Jim jumped into the air and swung Blackbeard's cutlass downwards at his father, but the pirate swerved left, his raven squawking and flying off, and Jim tumbled down the steps, landing with a bone-shaking *thud* back on deck.

The rats ran across the deck as Annie rushed at Jim, crawling on her hands and knees, snatching at the rats. They scurried out of her reach, so she grabbed Jim's ankles to yank him over to where his father stood.

Blackbeard slammed one huge, black boot down on Jim's chest.

Jim grabbed his father's boot with both hands. Gritting his teeth, he tried to lift it off his chest but it wouldn't move.

Slayne ran over. 'Um, Blackbeard, sir, you—'

'Not now, Slayne, you can see I'm in the middle of—'

'Yes, but, sir, I think yer really *should* see—'

'*Not now!*' Blackbeard hissed.

Jim winced under the weight of his father's boot, trying to slide it off him.

'Er, sir, yer really need to see this!' Slayne tugged at Blackbeard's jacket. 'I be pretty sure me eyes aren't deceivin' me, but there appears to be an, um . . . elephant,' the pirate captain squeaked, 'gallopin' towards us . . . over the surface of the ocean. And it has that bleedin' orange monkey on its back!'

'Orangutan!' Jim flipped his legs up between Blackbeard's, hammering his feet into the back of his father's knees. The pirate's legs buckled and he fell backwards, swinging his cutlass wildly. On his way down, Blackbeard sliced off Slayne's twine-tied 'two-beard' ponytails and Slayne grabbed at his chin in wide-eyed horror.

'No, no, not me beards! *Noooo!*'

Jim scrambled to his feet, winked at the three rats hiding in shadows by the broken mast, and ran to the ship's railings. Looking out to sea, with Rum, Flum and Sum joining him again, his jaw dropped open at the spectacle on the water below.

Bounding along on top of the ocean, as if she ran on the sea every day, he saw Elsa ploughing straight at the ship. Each of her four huge, elephant feet pounded up rings of water as she ran, lowering her head, her trunk and tusks before trumpet-roaring. Clutching her giant ears, Oskar waved a long, orange arm in the air and, echoing across the sea, Jim heard the familiar *wheeem-wheeem-wheeem* hum of the Narwhal tooth.

Jim watched as blubbery seal after blubbery seal sank below the water under the weight of each of

Elsa's thundering feet. She ran, using them as stepping stones, miles out from the island's shore, and each seal she stepped on dived beneath the surface and joined the front of a long floating blubber-raft.

'What is she . . . oh no . . .' Blackbeard was leaning on the railings now, next to Jim, his eyes widening as an elephant battering ram sped towards them. The pirate turned to the ship's crew, yelling, *'BRACE FOR IMPACT!'*

'How the *hell* can we do that hanging upside down?' one pirate yelled, but his words were drowned out by an ear-splitting, wood-crunch of a CRASH that thudded through the ship. From bow to stern, slats of deck bent and wobbled, the ship shifting sideways in the ocean like a bath toy smacked by a child.

Jim fell sideways into his father's arms. Stumbling backwards, Blackbeard could do nothing else but grab Jim in an odd, tight hug, stopping him from hitting the deck. And, for a moment, Jim and his father looked into each other's eyes.

The elephant slammed into the ship again.

Jim was thrown out of his father's grip as the ship trembled.

'These animals . . . they—'

'Were once your friends.' Oskar's orange hair dripped dark brown from the sea, and Jim jumped up and down at the sight of the orangutan clutching the ship's railings with his big, grey feet.

Blackbeard turned, slowly. 'Oskar.'

'So, it is true, Edward.' Oskar narrowed his eyes at the pirate, taking in the ship, Slayne, Annie, and all the pirates swinging upside down by their ankles. 'You *have* become the man I hoped you would not.'

The pirate grimaced. 'No one calls me Edward any more.'

Standing between his father and Oskar, Jim felt the air between them crackle, and the hairs on his neck rose.

'No,' Oskar said, pushing his little round glasses up his button nose, 'it would seem they do not.'

The orangutan jumped off the railing and looked up into the black-clad pirate's eyes. Jim could see Oskar was holding back tears.

'It is remarkable how humans reveal their story in their eyes. Their destiny is all written there, you just have to look deep enough.' Oskar turned to Jim and nodded, before turning back to Blackbeard. 'You, Edward, were full of energy and possibility. Sometimes I looked at you and thought you were like flicking to the back of a book to find out the ending, before you had read the whole story. And other times . . . I could see nothing in you. And that worried me.'

Blackbeard's cheek scar twitched. 'You have no idea who you're talking to.'

'Yes, I do.' Oskar walked right up to Jim's father, waving a small piece of wet paper in one hand. 'You are a man who did not try to be good. And so, I am afraid, you are a man who has already lost.'

Blackbeard chuckled and slid a pistol out of his chest belt, pointing it at Oskar. 'Your words mean nothing to me now, monkey.'

Jim bolted forward, but Oskar held up a hand to stop him.

Slayne and Annie watched their pirate king push out his chest and sneer down at the orangutan. 'You were right to be worried, because that snivelling, do-gooder of a sailor boy has gone. So, Oskar, say your prayers, or whatever it is vermin do before they die, because I'm taking my boy here with me to his destiny where he

228

will become—'

Oskar tenderly reached up and pressed a tiny old piece of paper against Jim's father's black shirt. From where he stood, Jim saw the note was faded and handwritten. It wasn't the WANTED parchment, this was a small personal note, signed by a human woman called Mary, and the only words Jim could make out, before Blackbeard snatched at the note, were: *And love him as much as I do.*

Jim's mouth went dry, and he felt dizzy. He knew who Mary must be.

'Now, Edward . . . Blackbeard . . . you will leave our island and not return. And you will tell your wife that her boy is safe and happy with his real family . . . here.' Oskar turned to Jim and held out one long-fingered hand. Jim grabbed it, and the orangutan brought him into his chest. Holding him tight, Oskar leapt across the deck, twirling them both around the rigging before landing back on the railings where he had arrived.

229

'Yes, Jim, that was a note from your mother,' the orang-utan said softly, 'and, again, I am sorry for keeping it from you.'

'Now I've met him,' he replied, nodding at his father, 'I can see why you did.'

The pair looked at one another as the three Rigging Rats ran up Jim's leg and onto his shoulder. He stroked them all one at a time, watching his father read the note, before the pirate dropped to his knees. The raven swooped down, landing on his master's shoulder.

Blackbeard wiped his mouth on his sleeve, his hollow eyes looking down at the pistol quivering in his hand.

The ship shunted violently again, a shockwave shooting up through Jim's legs.

'We had better go,' Oskar yelled, a roaring torrent of seawater falling from under the ship's hull below. 'You know I cannot swim, and the seals will not be able to hold Elsa's weight on the water's surface much longer!'

A loud trumpet from below, 'I heard that, *dear*!'

Jim glanced over the ship's side to see Elsa glaring up at him and Oskar, each of her feet standing on four, sinking seals.

'We have to go!' she yelled. 'I can swim, but not all that way back to shore!'

A white swell of water swirled around Elsa. There were seals and some other sleek shapes under the water. Jim couldn't make out what they were, but from up here he saw the ship was, somehow, floating *above* the ocean.

Oskar took a last look at Blackbeard kneeling on the deck.

'Ready to go home, Jim?' the orangutan asked.

Jim nodded. 'Yes, Oskar. Definitely.'

CHAPTER TWENTY-SEVEN

The orangutan somersaulted twice during the drop from the ship, before landing upright in a perfect sitting position on Elsa's neck. Trumpeting her delight, the elephant lifted up her front legs and turned back towards the island, the seals swimming beneath her feet.

Oskar glanced back up at Jim. 'Come on, *jump!*'

Looking into his friend's faraway eyes, and at the dark shadow of the island which kept changing position and disappearing with every deceptive lighthouse beam, Jim couldn't feel his legs. He *wanted* to jump, but he couldn't move.

The three rats were leaping up and down on his shoulder, nibbling his ears, yanking at his shirt, but he just . . . couldn't move. And all the sounds around him that he should be hearing – the yelling from upside-down pirates; the roiling seas; and the creaking ship rising into the air – he couldn't hear them.

His father was standing right beside him now. 'Having second thoughts, are we?'

Blackbeard's voice cut through Jim's mind, his body shaking as he watched, paralysed, whilst Elsa galloped back to the island on the seals. Her legs submerging, as the seals tired from carrying the weight, Jim knew she and Oskar had to go before they sank. He watched Oskar staring back at him as he and Elsa ran across the ocean.

The raven squawked at the Rigging Rats and they cowered against Jim's neck.

Feeling the rats' warmth on his skin, Jim snapped out of the trance, his limbs coming back to life.

'Oh no, not second thoughts,' he said, standing up tall, 'I just feel sorry for you and your crew, because I don't think you'll get very far back to your world with all those holes in the ship's hull.'

The pirate grabbed the railings, his knuckles turning white as he leant over to look at the sea below.

In a huge ring around the bottom of Slayne's ship,

were easily a hundred narwhals, flapping their tails wildly. Each of the white-black, speckled whales had impaled its long tusk *through* the ship's wooden hull and, collectively, they had all lifted it out of the ocean. With high-pitched *cleek-cleek-cleeks*, followed by *wheeem-wheeem-wheeem* wails echoing across and underwater, the narwhals carried the pirate ship away from the island.

Growling, Blackbeard stared at Jim. 'You and these vermin, you think you've won. But I assure you, my son, we are not done. We will never be done.'

Jim winced. 'We'll see,' he said, launching himself and the three rats backwards off the ship.

Jim sank underwater, ice-cold needles stabbing at his skin. Holding his breath as the surge of white water falling under the ship funnelled him backwards, he wrapped his hands around Rum, Flum and Sum, gripping them tight. His head broke the surface and he sucked in air. His mouth dropped open as he saw the thundering waterfall dropping off the ship's hull, from above, and swirling into an undercurrent of whirlpools that spat him far out behind the ship, amongst rolling wake waves.

Bobbing around, his teeth chattering, Jim plonked the three rats on his head as he was washed into the black, open ocean.

Jim couldn't see his father any more, but he imagined him, Slayne and Annie yelling down at the narwhals, utterly powerless to stop them carrying the ship away from the island.

The rats squeaked on Jim's head and, after a while, the ocean calmed and they swayed gently, watching the pirate ship sail away, hovering above the water, into the darkness.

Jim was shaking from the cold as he turned in the direction he *thought* the island was. He couldn't see it, meaning neither could his father or Slayne's crew, but as the long, jagged shape of Black Eel Rock loomed up ahead, he *should* be able to work out where he was.

Except, as he and the Rigging Rats floated on the ocean, the rock became huge and it blocked out the horizon. Jim could see the lighthouse beams sweeping across the sky, but out here they were . . . *confusing*. They came from many directions at once. He smiled, exasperated. The Espejo lens was doing its job well: hiding the island from him.

Jim kicked his legs underwater and the rats fidgeted on his head. Sighing, he wondered if what Slayne had said earlier was right – that there was no way he could swim all that way back to the island from this far out.

'I *can*,' he said, not giving in now and pulling in a breath to start swimming. He scanned the horizon but there was no sign of Elsa and Oskar on the ocean. If only he had jumped ship with them.

He lifted a trembling hand, which was turning blue, and stroked the three rats. They were all shivering, chittering to one another. Jim's skin tingled all over from the freezing water, and he was so tired. Everything began to fade to a grey colour, and he could . . . barely . . . stop . . . his face from dropping into the ocean. 'It's all right, y-you three . . . but I . . . d-don't think . . . I can s-stay awake—'

'CHEESY . . . TOAD . . . FEET!' A familiar voice blasted in his ear, echoing across the bay.

Jim snapped his head back up.

'*TUMBLING ... ROTTEN ... MANGOES!*' Floating next to Jim's shoulder was the 208-year-old turtle, Trent. The turtle butted his head into Jim's face, nudging him sideways.

The three Rigging Rats leapt on to the turtle's huge shell, swinging one another around happily.

Jim smiled, hugging the old turtle's wrinkly neck. 'Oh Trent! I can't begin to tell you—'

'*WHAT? ... SPEAK ... UP!*' The turtle swished his giant flipper-paddles in the water, gliding in front of Jim.

'I said,' Jim clamped his freezing, blue hands onto Trent's neck and, his breath a white mist, pulled his heavy body up on to the turtle's shell, 'TAKE US HOME.'

Silence.

'*SHOULDN'T ... BE ... HERE!*' yelled Trent, and he swept his flippers backwards in the ocean, heaving them forward. '*TAKING ... YOU ... HOME!*'

Still shivering, Jim knelt up on the turtle's shell holding on to Rum, Flum and Sum as they huddled together. Black Eel Rock floated by and soon, after they'd drifted through beam three-and-a-half's lens

237

mirage barrier around the shoreline, the black shape of the island emerged. And, on top of it, standing tall with its beams sweeping across the ocean's night sky, was Jim's home.

Trent covered the stretch of water to the island in no time, its silhouette becoming more defined, with dark cliffs, swaying grass on the fields above, and a moonlit Seal Cove appearing out of the night haze. Being so close to home, after everything, Jim stopped shivering. He felt warmer.

Sssssssshhhhh.

Trent slid out of the water, up onto the sand.

The Rigging Rats jumped off his back, scampering up the beach, as Jim gave the giant turtle a big, heavy kiss on the top of his wrinkly, brown head.

'Thank you, Trent.' Jim rolled off the turtle's shell, onto the sand. He pushed Trent back into the sea and the turtle splashed his flippers in the water, springing around to head back out.

'INVADING . . . PIRATE . . . NUMBSKULLS!'

Pausing, Jim watched the turtle go and realised what Trent had been saying . . . he'd *known*. All along.

Jim chuckled and, dripping wet, he turned to see the shadow of an orangutan standing on the beach. His lip quivered.

Oskar stepped out of the darkness and curled his long arm around him. Jim squeezed him, hard, and they stayed that way for a while, before Oskar held him out in front of him by his shoulders. The orangutan smiled.

'You made the right choice. You saved our island from pirates and you saved all our lives too. Come now, we should get you warmed up and then we must celebrate!'

Oskar led Jim along the cove shoreline, seals *arf-arfing* nearby, and the two of them wound their way up the cliff path to the lighthouse.

In the distance, Jim could see the silhouettes of all his friends waiting by the lighthouse door. An elephant, a raccoon, three rats, a beetle mother and her babies, a cat, a millipede and—

Tallulah squawked as she landed on Jim's shoulder, the parrot nuzzling her beak into his ear. 'Welcome home,' she said, flapping her bright red-green-blue wings, slapping him in the face.

Jim smiled, stroking Tallulah's head feathers as he and Oskar strolled by the cliff edge, towards the others. The lighthouse beams swept over them into the night sky.

One, two, three, three-and-a-half.

Oskar stopped walking and looked out to sea and Jim paused next to him, staring at the bright moon.

'We know they will be back,' the orangutan whispered. 'They will find *some* way to see the island again. And when they do come, there will be many, *many* more of them.'

Jim nodded, swallowing.

Oskar pushed his glasses up his button nose. 'They will be worse, too. Much worse.'

'I know.' Jim brushed up against the orangutan's arm. 'But, when they come, when my father returns, we'll be ready.'

Oskar knocked Jim's hat off his head, chuckling, and Jim caught it just before it landed on Maximus.

Laughing merrily, the orangutan leapt up onto the outside of the lighthouse's doorframe. His long toes gripping the frame's metal top, he leaned flat against the building's stone for a moment, before jumping up and across to a tiny porthole window a few feet away.

Swinging around the circular casing, Oskar spider-jumped thirty feet straight up to the next porthole window.

Jim and the other animals watched, open-mouthed, as their orangutan friend repeated these vertical leaps as if climbing a giant, branchless redwood tree, until he finally somersaulted over the Lantern Room balcony and disappeared.

'Show off,' said Rafi.

A moment later a *whooom-whooom-whooom* sound echoed down from the lighthouse's top.

Jim stared up at the night sky, watching Oskar spin the Narwhal tusk, silhouetted against the moon.

Wheeem-wheeem-wheeem.

After a few moments, the grass around Jim began rustling. Then he heard screeches in the sky, splashing from out across the ocean, *aarf-aarf-aarfs* from the seals, and the thunder of . . .

He turned to see a herd of deer galloping towards them, the first of them skidding to a stop on the lighthouse front lawn, looking at Jim with night-sparkles in their eyes.

Then flamingos from the Flaming Forest colony flew down on to the lighthouse lawn. Otters, armadillos, lemurs and gophers came running, followed by bog moles and termites, bats and glow-worms. Every type of seagull squawked overhead and even penguins from the small, separate northern needle-island, the Penguin Perch, came. So did the six Totem Birds that lived in the dead and burnt branches of the lightning-struck Charcoal Tree, each of them landing on Elsa's head and sitting on top of one another, their heads in a vertical line.

Beyond the lawn – where Jim was spinning in

circles, smiling – and out in the sea surrounding the island, orcas, dolphins, whales, octopus and jellyfish swam near the shore, and the old turtle, Trent, popped his head up too.

And, as all the bugs from the lighthouse basement – including the beetle mother and her babies – spread out across the grass and beneath his feet, and with Elsa, Rafi, Tallulah, Claudette, Maximus and the Rigging Rats beside him, Jim knew *this* was where he belonged. With his real family.

THE END.

FOR NOW.

ACKNOWLEDGMENTS

Writing a book is like being the captain of a pirate ship. The author, that's me, decides the direction to sail in – towards adventures, danger and magic – and my amazing crewmates help with the journey by pointing out when we're navigating in the wrong direction so we can, like any good explorers, try a route with calmer seas.

I have some talented crewmates who helped me bring *The Animal Lighthouse* to life. First is my Quartermaster, Bella Pearson of Guppy Books. Bella has been a guiding force, editor supremo, and all-round supportive publisher. Thank you, Bella, for believing in me and this story.

My First Mate on board is the creative wonderment of an illustrator, Ciara Flood, who turned my characters and settings into her beautiful, olde-worlde, vibrant and fun drawings.

Other Guppy crewmates to thank are Ness Wood for her design direction in steering the ship's look; Liz Scott as the PR Adviser-in-Chief; Hannah Featherstone and Nicki Marshall; Catherine Alport and all the Michael O'Mara sales team.

With me, on this journey, for so long was Amy Garrett. Thank you Amy for being my number one reader, supporter, best friend, and for the magical times we spent together.

Thank you Craig Robb, my lifelong shipmate, for your wisdom, belief and for helping me crack the lighthouse mirage illusion. Thank you Katie and Pippin too!

When I started out on this piratical adventure, it began with the help of The Golden Egg Academy and the inspiring guidance of Imogen Cooper. Thank you Imogen – you always knew that me breaking your garden gate would eventually be repaid with me 'breaking into' publishing, right? And thank you to the wonderful friendship of author Vanessa Harbour. To Abi Fionnghuala Kohlhoff. To Ben Illis. And to Barry Cunningham!

Writer, illustrator, agent, and publisher friends have all joined the crew and been a huge, encouraging family. Firstly, there's James Nicol. A wonderful wrangler of witches and very special, supportive friend. Then there's award-winning, inspiro-author and all-round positive force of a friend, Vashti Hardy. Jan Dunning and Emma Perry for the love and support. Big hugs to Lorraine Gregory, Jennifer Killick, Andrew Wright, Beverley Birch, K.L Kettle, Jane Martin, Annaliese Avery, Charlotte Teeple-Salas, Emma Greenwood, Karen Minto, Ele Nash, Tracy Darnton, Lynette Fisher, Cat Black, Clare Helen Welsh, Cathie Kelly, and Bex Nunn.

Then there are my wonderful group of writer friends: Jenny Rees, Kay Weetch, Andrea Fazackerley, Maurice Lyon, Miriam Craig, John Malone, Glyn Scott, Chrissie Sains, George Poles, Aliss Michele, Trudie Thomas, Anne-Marie Stone, Barbara-Ann Jones, Becky Hamilton, Olivia Wakeford, Victoria Bennion, Lisa Emily Wakely, Karen Thirkell, Tamsin Cooke, BeeBee Taylor, and Lucy Coats.

There are *hundreds* more fantastic Golden Egg friends I've missed out here, but there isn't the space. Sending you all big, pirate-y hugs!

Wonderful SCBWI people, thank you! Especially Elaine Cline and Sarah Broadley.

Society of Authors – especially Bryony Hall – you guys are the best.

To all the librarians, teachers, TAs, youth workers, mums, dads, grans, grandads, aunts, uncles, booksellers and bloggers – I salute your hard work, passion and dedication to helping children and young people enjoy reading.

Thank you Dan Lane for setting me on a new path to writing children's books. Thanks Mum, for buying that typewriter toy when I was five years old and introducing me to my love of the sea and lighthouses. And to my dad, Fulvia, my brother, Matthew, and Robin for their love. And to everyone else in my family.

Thank you Kate Spurrier, for all the uplifting and supportive talks.

Thanks to my American, Canadian, Devon, Portsmouth and Bristol friends and book love to my Edinburgh Book Festival friends, and to all the amazing and talented author friends I am lucky to have. This includes the brilliant Cathy Cassidy (and Liam) for spending many kind hours helping me reach this point.

Every ship needs a cat, and my black cat Watson is on board and has been a tireless companion and consultant for some of the animals here on the island (especially Claudette). We miss Sherlock, Watson's brother, very much.

Thanks to Stephen King.

And, last but most definitely not least, to the most important crewmates on this ship. You, the Reader. Thank you for picking up my book and reading it. I hope you enjoyed the story, and are looking forward to sailing with me again soon!

Until next time.

Anthony

Anthony Burt

Anthony Burt has worked in primary, secondary and adult education, and ran inspiring community youth work, art, music, film and TV projects for children with special needs for 20 years. He's a professional slime-maker, teacher and bookseller, and in 2019 he helped entertain 8000 children in 20 days as host of the Imagination Lab at the Edinburgh International Book Festival. Anthony enjoys writing all kinds of children's stories, usually with a dark but heart-warming and comedic twist. Anthony is an eternally faithful concierge to his cat Watson and lives in Frome.

Ciara Flood

Ciara grew up in the Middle East and Ireland. She studied Visual Communications at Dublin Institute of Technology and after graduating worked as a graphic designer. She now lives with her partner and their two children in London where she works as a freelance illustrator and designer. Ciara is the author/illustrator of picture books *Those Pesky Rabbits*, *The Perfect Picnic* and *There's a Walrus in My Bed*. She draws all her illustrations in pencil or ink before using a mixture of watercolour and Photoshop for the final artwork.

www.ciaraflood.co.uk